ACADEMIA NUTS

Also by Charles R. Larson:

THE EMERGENCE OF AFRICAN FICTION

AFRICAN SHORT STORIES (Editor)

PREJUDICE: TWENTY TALES OF OPPRESSION
    AND LIBERATION (Editor)

OPAQUE SHADOWS AND OTHER AFRICAN STORIES (Editor)

THE NOVEL IN THE THIRD WORLD

Academia Nuts

or,
The Collected Works
of Clara LePage
by
Charles R. Larson

the bobbs-merrill company, inc.
indianapolis/new york

Designed by Jerry W. Byers
Manufactured in the United States of America

First printing

Library of Congress Cataloging in Publication Data

Larson, Charles R
  Academia nuts.

  I. Title.
PZ4.L3358Ac [PS3562.A752]   813'.5'4   76-46698
ISBN 0-672-52310-8

Excerpts from this book originally appeared (in somewhat different
form) in the following publications: *The Atlantic Monthly*, *Colorado
Quarterly*, *The Saturday Review*, *Negro American Literature Forum*, *The
CEA Critic*, *The CEA Forum*, *The New England Review*, *Pucred*, *The
Literary Review*, *Twigs*, *The Use of English*, *PMLA*, and *Studies in
Contemporary Satire.*

PERMISSIONS

"Confounding Sophocles," copyright © 1971, 1977.
"Come to the Ship, Leggatt, Honey," copyright © 1968, 1977.
"Lady Macbeth's Pregnancy," copyright © 1977.
"*The Oxford English Dictionary*—A Negative Note," copyright ©
    1972 by *Pucred*, reprinted with their permission.
"Portrait of Henry James as a Young Lady," reprinted from *The
    Literary Review* (Fall 1973, Volume 17, Number 1), published by
    Fairleigh Dickinson University, Rutherford, N.J.
"Dame Van Winkle's Burden," copyright © 1969, 1977.

A NOTE OF THANKS

Teaching is never an isolated experience. The ideas for several of these dialogues were suggested by a number of my colleagues and friends. My thanks especially to Faye Kelly, for the anecdote that led to "Confounding Sophocles"; to Shirley Yarnall for "J. Alfred Prufrock and the Prostitute"; and to Nancy Carter Goodley for "Coleridge's Ancient Mariner and Freud's Missing Complex." I would also like to express my appreciation to C. Michael Curtis, at *The Atlantic Monthly,* for publishing the first of these dialogues; to Dick Jesson, the editor of *Pucred,* who encouraged me to keep writing them; and to Doris Grumbach and Maurice English, for their early support and enthusiasm for the book-length project that eventually evolved.

To Her,
and to my colleagues

CONTENTS

PART ONE · · ·
GREAT BOOKS (Spring)
Confounding Sophocles   3
Come to the Ship, Leggatt, Honey   10
Lady Macbeth's Pregnancy   16
The Oxford English Dictionary—
    A Negative Note   23
Portrait of Henry James as a Young Lady   30
Ibsen's *Ghosts* and Interdisciplinary Studies   36

PART TWO · · ·
AMERICAN LITERATURE (Fall/Spring)
Dame Van Winkle's Burden   43
Poe's Raven—The Last Word   49
Strange Goings On at Walden Pond   54
Hester Prynne and the Pill   60
Moby Dick and Sexless Politics   68
Leaves of Grass—Pure Acapulco Gold   74
The Secret Life of Huckleberry Finn   81
Will the Real Emily Dickinson
    Please Stand Up?   87
The Deification of Booker T. Washington   92
J. Alfred Prufrock and the Prostitute   97
A Farewell to Hemingway's What?   102

PART THREE · · ·
    MAJOR BRITISH WRITERS (Fall/Spring)
Beowulf's Hangup   111
Key to *The Canterbury Tales*   117
How Shakespeare Wrote His Sonnets   124
What Really Happens in *Hamlet?*   130
Archetypal Patterns in *The MLA Style Sheet*   137
Return to *Paradise Lost* Revisited   144
Coleridge's "Ancient Mariner" and Freud's
    Missing Complex   150
Coleridge's "Ancient Mariner" and the
    Skinner Box   156
Cliff's Notes—The Archetypal Victorian Novel 160
Browning's Last Duchess and the
    Weight-Watcher's Diet   165
Academia Nuts   171

PART ONE

Great Books
(spring)

Confounding Sophocles

"I don't see any real evidence," she began, "that Oedipus was actually sleeping with his mother."

I looked up from my notes to see who had spoken, somewhat surprised that it was the new girl who had added my Great Books seminar at the beginning of the hour. It was the last class of the second week of the spring semester (the final day for adding or dropping a class), and I was annoyed that students were still changing their schedules. She looked about seventeen or eighteen years old.

"You what?" I stammered, shuffling the index cards in front of me until I found the one she had filled in. On it, in green felt pen, in perfect penmanship, she had written:

LePage, Clara R.
Anderson Hall 402
Phone: 254-7018
Sophomore
Major: Business

"I don't think that *Oedipus* is about what you say it is," she replied. Then she added, obviously embarrassed by what she'd said, "I mean, I think you've misunderstood some of the story."

"Have you read the work?" I couldn't help asking her. "Didn't you just add this course today?"

"I read the play last night," she replied; then added, "David Epstein told me what the assignment was."

"Who's he?" I asked her, wondering if I was in the right classroom. I waited for her reply while she lit a cigarette.

"He was taking this course. He wanted me to tell you that he's dropped it."

Epstein? David Epstein? I flipped through the index cards again until I found his name.

"Oh, yes. You say he's no longer enrolled in this course?" I asked her.

"He decided to take Photography," she replied.

"Now where were we, Miss— Miss—"

"LePage," she replied.

"Yes, now where were we, Miss LePage?" I asked her. "You were saying something about the incest theme, as I remember."

"I said I don't think that Oedipus was actually sleeping with his mother."

"What do you mean, Miss LePage—that they had twin beds or separate bedrooms or what?" I asked, trying to lighten the atmosphere in the room. I wondered if Miss LePage was old enough to know what she was talking about.

"No, not exactly, though that, of course, is possible. What I mean is that I don't think Oedipus was really *sleeping* with her." She hesitated a moment before adding, "I don't think anything was going on. I doubt if there was any sex involved."

How, I ask you, was I supposed to reply to that?

"Miss LePage," I began a moment later, after I had collected my thoughts, "don't you think your statement is difficult to substantiate in light of several thousand years of reactions to Sophocles' drama? Without the whole incest theme, Sophocles wouldn't have written his play, would he?"

"That's what bothers me," she replied. "I don't understand how people can be so confused in their interpretations. You'd think that they'd been reading some other work or something."

"Have you?" I couldn't resist asking.

"No, just Sophocles. That's why I don't understand the reasons people think this is such a good play. There's a flaw in the whole thing, and I can't seem to find anyone who's noticed it in all these years."

"Would you mind enlightening the rest of us?" I asked, beginning to lose my patience. I wasn't at all certain that she had read *Oedipus*—unless maybe the *Masterplots* version.

Miss LePage puffed away at her cigarette, trying to gain the attention of the rest of the students. (Not that she didn't already have it.) Then she continued, "Well, it's all quite obvious to me. Oedipus had simply been

living with his mother, but they weren't sleeping together. It was purely a platonic affair, you might say."

"But how can you be certain?" I asked, almost
pleading with her to get to the facts. "Give us some proof
from the text to support what you're saying."

"It's clear to me that if Oedipus and Jocasta were
sharing the same bed, either Jocasta was blind or
Oedipus always slept with his socks on."

"I don't think they wore socks in those days, Miss
LePage," I said a little sarcastically, as I watched her
exhale several dainty puffs of smoke.

"Well, something's really fishy here, and that's why
I don't think they could possibly have been sleeping
together."

"Why, Miss LePage? Why, why, why?" Her obfus-
cation was becoming infuriating.

"Well, if you recall, Oedipus's feet were supposed to
have been bound in a special way when he was a child, so
that there were special markings on them. His parents
had that done to him. Didn't Jocasta ever look at his feet?
Even once, perhaps? Can they have been sleeping together all those years without Jocasta's ever looking
down at her husband's feet? I mean, I'm not trying to
imply that she was some kind of foot fetishist or anything,
but how can you sleep with someone for twenty years and
not once notice his feet? That isn't even normal, is it?"

I stood there thunderstruck. Two thousand five
hundred years and no one had ever noticed this inconsistency in the play.

"Miss LePage, is this the first time you've ever read
Oedipus?" I asked her.

"No, of course not. I read it in high school."

"You mean that this idea of yours—or whatever you

call it—was something your high school teacher told you?"

"No, she thought the same thing you do. I just discovered the feet problem last night when I was reading the play again. David Epstein gave me his copy of the book, since he won't be needing it any longer."

"You're a business major, Miss LePage?" I asked her, glancing down at her card once again.

"Yes—advance placement," she replied.

"What do you mean?"

"Well, this is my first year at the university, but it's my sophomore year because of all the credits I got for taking the exams they give at the placement office."

"Oh. Then why are you taking this class?"

"They told me yesterday that I shouldn't take four business courses in one semester. I needed a humanities course, so I decided to add this one."

"Well, that's very interesting, Miss LePage. Very interesting. Perhaps all of us should have a little more variety in our backgrounds. I sometimes have the feeling that those of us who are in the humanities can no longer see the forest for the trees—if you'll excuse the expression."

I looked around the classroom at the other students, but they didn't give any evidence of having heard what I'd said. "Was there anything else you wanted to add to your interpretation?" I was hoping she was finished so I could return to the security of my office and reread Sophocles' play to see if I could discover why such an oversight had never been detected before. I was hoping it was simply that we'd been reading a poor translation.

"Well, there isn't too much to add, except, of course, that this doesn't especially help Freud's theory of

7

the Oedipus complex. Since Oedipus was living with Jocasta, and since she must have noticed his feet right at the beginning, we have to conclude that she realized Oedipus was her son. So we can't say that Oedipus had an Oedipus complex, but that Jocasta was the one with the Oedipus complex."

Surely she hadn't said what I thought she'd said! Where the devil had she ever learned all these things?

"I don't deny that Oedipus killed his father," she continued, "or that he was married to Jocasta, his mother. That I think is all pretty well established. All I'm saying is that the two of them weren't having any sexual relationship per se. My guess is either that Oedipus suffered some injury along the way—perhaps in that fight with his father, or that besides having his ankles pierced, something else was done to him as a child."

"Then why in heaven's name does he continue living with Jocasta all those years, and why does she continue living with him?"

"Well, of course, Oedipus doesn't realize that he's living with his mother. She's the only one who knows that," Miss LePage replied. "It's all pretty much a matter of saving one's face. After all, Oedipus is supposed to be a great man—solving the riddle of the Sphinx and all that—a hero. He's simply a hero with everyone but his wife—or in this case his mother. You see, she's been able to fulfill every mother's secret dream—she's never had to give her son up."

"There's a little problem here, Miss LePage. You've forgotten about the children—the four children of Oedipus and Jocasta. How do you account for them?"

"That's easy. Jocasta's fertility has never been in doubt. It's simply that Oedipus isn't the father."

"Who is, then?"

"Creon."

"Creon—Jocasta's brother?" I asked her.

"Of course, I didn't say the incest theme was missing from the play—it's just that people haven't noticed who's really involved. After all, if Sophocles didn't include a little sensationalism in his drama, how was he going to make any money with it?"

"Miss LePage, could I see you for a few minutes at the end of the class?"

Come to the Ship,
Leggatt, Honey

Although I tried to convince Miss LePage to drop the course, I wasn't successful. Her advisor, she said, had insisted that she take the freshman Great Books course—and mine was the only section she could fit into her schedule. "I'm afraid you'll be awfully bored," I said to her, after talking to her for a few minutes. I had concluded, however, that she was one of the best-read business majors I had ever encountered. "You've probably already read a third of the books."

"Oh, that's all right," she replied. "That'll just give me more time to study for my other courses."

"Some books are worth reading a second time," I replied. Then I tried another tactic: "Since you're already a sophomore, wouldn't you rather take an advanced literature class instead of this one? Most students take this course to fulfill their freshman English requirement."

She reminded me that it was the last day for adding or dropping classes, and since it was late in the afternoon, we decided to leave it at that.

When she didn't show up for the next class, I thought maybe she had changed her mind. No such luck, however. At the following class, on Joseph Conrad's novella, *The Secret Sharer*, there she was with an armful of heavy economics textbooks. What surprised me was that she didn't say a word throughout the entire class. I began to wonder if, in fact, she now realized that the course was too elementary for her. She just sat there smoking one cigarette after another (Gauloises, I noticed).

It had been a particularly difficult class to get through, and I would have welcomed her comments. No one seemed to want to say anything, though one young man seemed to be so concerned with taking notes that his pen never stopped scratching at a large yellow pad. At the end of the class, I wanted to try to sum up my ideas, but something made me ask if anyone had anything he wanted to say.

"I think you've missed the whole point," Miss Le Page blurted out, without waiting for me to call on her. It was then that I noticed her appearance. She had bright red hair, and she wasn't wearing blue jeans like all the rest of the female students. She was, in fact, rather attractive, though terribly young.

"How?" I asked, glancing at the young man sitting

across the table from her. He was still scribbling on his yellow pad of paper. It looked as if his pen would never stop.

"They're gay."

"Who?" I asked, looking for reactions from the class. There were none.

"The Captain, at least—Leggatt, too. Though he's not such a clear case."

"How do you know?" I asked her, wondering how she'd come up with such an interpretation. There were six more minutes before the bells would ring.

"The pajamas," Miss LePage replied; "sharing the pajamas. That's where the title comes in—that's what they're really sharing."

"Tops or bottoms?" another student asked, perking up a little, looking at me as if I hadn't heard of homosexuals.

"It doesn't matter," Miss LePage replied. "The point is they're always whispering to each other, sharing pajamas, hiding from the others on the ship."

I fumbled with my copy of *The Secret Sharer*, nervously wondering how she had arrived at her interpretation.

"The Captain's the queer one," Miss LePage continued. "Leggatt only puts up with it until he can get away from the ship." There were a couple of snickers from the class. "That's why he left the *Sephora* in the first place—they were all gay on that ship. Leggatt killed one of the crew who'd made advances to him. Remember, Leggatt was on his first voyage; his father was a minister."

"That's right," the young man sitting next to Miss LePage agreed. I looked at the boy with the yellow pad.

There was an audible scratching noise from his fountain
pen whenever Miss LePage wasn't speaking.

"Don't you see it, sir?" she asked me, looking at the
rest of the class. Several other students nodded their
heads; I wondered if there was some kind of conspiracy.

"Go on," I said, "I'm listening."

"Well, there isn't much else. It's all fairly
obvious—it's in my paper there—that sitting on the john
in the bathroom and all that. Poor Leggatt, trying to get
away from the Captain. How'd you like to spend all that
time sitting on the john?"

"Bit of an inconvenience," I muttered, feeling
sweat break out on my forehead. Everyone in the class
was looking at me, waiting to hear what I'd say.

"It's the Captain," Miss LePage continued, stop-
ping a minute to light another cigarette. "Why else do
you think the crew hate him? They happen to be fairly
normal on his ship. Unfortunately, Leggatt swims to the
wrong ship—that's the irony of it all—where the Captain's gay. But this time he knows he'll have to put up
with it or he'll lose his neck. So he waits till he can swim
ashore and has to sit in the john all day long so he won't be
discovered. The crew would probably kill him. It's
purely Freudian. No reason to tell the crew that their
Captain's gay—they already know it. Why do you think
he was up there on deck alone in the first place? With the
ladder over the edge, just in case some nice young man
happened to be swimming by. How terribly conven-
ient."

The bells on the quad began to chime. I looked at
the boy with the yellow pad. His right hand was covered
with black ink, which had run all over the pad and the
table. He looked a little as if he had wet his pants.

"Well, that's all very interesting, Miss LePage," I said, getting up from the table. "We'll continue this next time." I edged my way around the room, managing to leave before any of the students. I wanted to get back to my office and read Miss LePage's paper—to see how far she'd erred.

It was all fairly obvious, all there in surprisingly concise English prose. Leggatt, the Captain, the pajamas, the whispering, sitting on the john all day long—which was better than what happened at night— proper footnotes, virtually no errors (one comma splice, one misspelled word). All clear except for the end, the last page, which was missing from her paper. Her essay ended, "Thus Leggatt's search for identity leads him into the depths of human perversity, but the waters of the sea act as a baptism in—" and there the sentence was broken.

I was distressed. I wanted to find out how Miss LePage had ended her paper. It was impossible to give her a grade unless I had that last page. She had completely ignored so many facets of Conrad's tale—the "floppy hat" that saves Leggatt's life, for instance—she had used only those aspects that could be twisted to fit her own demented interpretation. I knew she couldn't explain the function of the hat, but I'd have to wait until Friday to find out what else she'd written.

Friday I was early, but Miss LePage was late, so I had to wait until the end of the period, after our initial discussion of Dante's *Divine Comedy*, before I could talk to her. Did she think Dante was gay also? (No, but Beatrice was obviously sexually frigid.) What had happened to the last page of her paper on *The Secret Sharer*? She'd discovered it in her typewriter but had forgotten to

14

bring it to class. She'd bring it the next time. Could she explain the meaning of the hat floating in the sea at the end of the story?

"It's perfectly obvious. Leggatt didn't want to keep anything that reminded him of the Captain. He left it floating in the sea purposely. It was a woman's hat," Miss LePage confessed.

"A woman's hat?"

"Of course, a bonnet, so it would keep the sun from his eyes. A mere fetish. Belonged to the Captain's aunt. The Captain was a transvestite, you know."

Lady Macbeth's Pregnancy

"I think you're coming down way too hard on Lady Macbeth," Miss LePage said, interrupting my introductory comments on the play.

It was the seventh week of the semester, and I had learned a number of interesting things about Miss Le Page. She was, as I had guessed, only seventeen years old, but her reading had been so voracious that I could rarely make a reference to any literary work that she wasn't already familiar with. She claimed a preference for modern literature over the classics, stating one day after class that she'd "had enough of books like the *Odyssey* and the *Idiocy*." Furthermore, it was quite ap-

16

parent that she was the only student in the class who read critical commentaries about the literary works we discussed each week, though, with her literal-mindedness, these were not always that helpful.

"Lady Macbeth's not any of those things at all. Shakespeare intended her to be regarded sympathetically. You're not giving her a chance. If you weren't a man, you wouldn't call her all those things."

"All I said, Miss LePage, is that in *Macbeth* there are two kinds of female characters—witches and bitches. It's up to you to decide in which category she belongs."

"Neither," she replied. "And don't tell me I'm trying to push Women's Lib, because Lady Macbeth isn't that kind of woman either. If she were alive today, I doubt if she'd subscribe to *Ms.*"

"What is she, then, Miss LePage?" I asked her, looking at the other students to see how they were reacting to her comments.

"She's simply an average human being—but a woman made neurotic by psychoanalysis, you might say. If Freud and Company had left her alone, our understanding of the play would be much more realistic. She's not neurotic; she doesn't wash her hands because of bad toilet training; she's not suffering from any guilt complexes; she's not even trying to wear the pants in Macbeth's household. She's a victim of circumstance—a victim of something she can't handle."

"Penis envy?" I asked her, thinking it was the one area she might possibly have overlooked.

She ignored my comment.

"Everything she does is done to alter these circumstances."

"Such as?"

17

"The banquet scene—Banquo's ghost, for example. Have you ever wondered why Macbeth's the only one who sees Banquo's ghost?"

"What does that have to do with it?" I asked her.

"Well, that scene proves she's not the guilty one. If she were as evil as the critics have pointed out, wouldn't she also see the ghost?" She continued before I could say anything. "There, you see. She isn't as wicked as everyone says she is. She may have been involved in some shady deals, but Shakespeare wants us to believe that that side of her personality has been brought about solely by her attempt to escape from a terrible marriage. I think it's even possible that the whole ghost scene was staged by Lady Macbeth to drive her husband insane. When that doesn't work, she decides to leave him."

"I think you've lost me, Miss LePage."

"All right, let me start again. The play is about accidental power. Both of them—Macbeth and Mrs. Macbeth—are victims of circumstance. They weren't educated to be royalty, and when they become king and queen, they don't know how to use the power in their hands. That's what's so significant about the play, Professor. That's why it says something for us today."

"Ah, you mean *Macbird*—Lyndon Johnson and Lady Bird?" I asked her, recalling the lampoonery of that version.

"Perhaps, though I'd say that the situation Shakespeare created holds true for any number of other cases also."

"You mean that Lady Macbeth's worthy of our sympathy?"

"In a way. She's like any woman who feels that she's

been ignored by her husband. What I'm saying is that Lady Macbeth has been tromped on by the critics for three hundred and fifty years; she's become a kind of scapegoat. She doesn't have all those hangups. She's not that screwed up at all. It's the critics who have the hangups. I'm willing to bet you that most of them hated their mothers. Lady Macbeth's basically a good person, a sympathetic woman, a typical female. She may be ambitious, but her ambition is the result of being fettered to an incompetent man. She's married a dullard, but unfortunately she doesn't realize this until the string of violent events begins—the murders. So all she can do after that is try to escape from Macbeth's demands. When this doesn't work, there's little left for her to do but leave him—but that isn't as easy as it seems." She stopped for a minute and tried to light a cigarette, but she couldn't get her lighter to work.

"Aren't you getting rather far removed from the realities of Shakespeare's play, Miss LePage?" I asked her.

"Not at all. These are all important aspects of the play that need to be understood. Lady Macbeth has normal desires; all she needs is a little kindness and understanding from her husband, but she never really gets it. When placed next to the rest of Shakespeare's female characters, she comes off quite positively. She's not insipid like Ophelia or Cordelia; she's not a monster like Regan or Goneril. Her sole problem is that she's married to Macbeth, and he doesn't give a damn about her. If she suffers from anything, it's insecurity because of her looks. The hand-washing scene, for example, doesn't have a thing to do with the murders. It's much more basic than that." She tapped the unlit cigarette on the table, as if she were keeping time to some unheard music.

"You mean she's got dishpan hands?" I asked her, hoping to rouse a chuckle from the other students. (I didn't.)

"No, it's just a birthmark or a skin infection. The entire dish-washing—I mean hand-washing—scene was put in the play for comic relief, never to be taken seriously. Shakespeare's father, if you recall, was a glovemaker. If Lady Macbeth had worn gloves, she wouldn't have had to worry about the appearance of her hands, but since she wasn't brought up as royalty, she never learned this. Audiences probably rolled in the aisles when they first saw the play; it's only the later readers who have failed to notice the comic overtones of the scene. Shakespeare put a commercial for gloves right in the middle of his play. He was poking fun at the *nouveau* royalty. The whole problem could have been solved by a pair of inexpensive gloves."

"Somehow, Miss LePage, I think you've let your business background influence your interpretation."

"No, I'm serious about this, Professor. Lady Macbeth's problem is heightened by the fact that even if she manages to get free of her husband, she's still got the problems of approaching middle age. She's getting heavier and she's concerned about her appearance." She continued to fidget with the unlit cigarette.

"Miss LePage, one of us has got to be crazy. How did you ever come to the conclusion that Lady Macbeth is putting on weight?" I asked her. "How did you ever come to *any* of these conclusions?"

"It's right there in the text of the play, Professor.

When she says, 'O! that this too too solid flesh would melt.' Don't you think that's rather obvious? What she needs are some good diuretics. Although I think there's another interpretation of that line. If critics—"

"Miss LePage," I interrupted her, "I hate to tell you this, but you've got the wrong play. Lady Macbeth doesn't say that. It's Hamlet who says that line!"

That didn't stop her. "Oh, I must have got them confused. I read all of Shakespeare's tragedies over the weekend before I wrote my paper, so I could place Lady Macbeth in perspective with Shakespeare's other female characters. But that really doesn't change much. If you remember, she keeps repeating the word 'heavy.' You'd be shocked too if you were forty-some years old and just discovered you were pregnant for the first time, wouldn't you?"

"Pregnant? Where does it say that?"

"It's a matter of having all her dreams destroyed. Critics are always trying to figure out how many children Lady Macbeth had. The fact is that she's just become pregnant for the first time. All her life she's wanted to be a mother, never really thinking that she would be, and now that she's pregnant, her husband's on an ego-trip to become king. They're simply a mismatched pair; he's interested in power, she's interested in pregnancy."

"Miss LePage, there's no evidence for any of this in the play anywhere. You're basing your entire interpretation on that one word 'heavy.' Heavy probably had nothing to do with being pregnant in those days. Why didn't you look it up in the *OED?*"

"What's that?"—breaking the unlit cigarette in two.

"The *Oxford English Dictionary*. It lists the origins of words and all their changing meanings down through

21

the years. If you look up a word like 'heavy,' you can see what it meant during Shakespeare's time."

"All right, but even if it didn't mean pregnant, the fundamental problem is that Lady Macbeth's real desire is to be more fully appreciated by the men in her life. And that desire accounts for almost all of her actions in the play—especially the last two acts and the sleepwalking scene, a kind of feigned madness."

"You haven't confused her with Hamlet again, have you?" I asked her.

"No, not this time. The proof is at the end of the play. First, there's the sleepwalking scene, which is intended to act as a cover-up for what's about to happen. All of this is faked so she can get away from Macbeth, who she now realizes was never interested in her in the first place."

"You've completely lost me. I don't know what you're talking about."

"Lady Macbeth's plans to get away from her husband. She fakes the sleepwalking, and when that doesn't get her anywhere she pretends that she's killed herself."

"Now tell me, Miss LePage, how can she pretend to kill herself? How can anyone pretend to kill himself?"

"It's very simple. Word is brought to Macbeth that his wife is dead, but there's never any real proof of that—we never see the body, as we do later with Macbeth. And Macbeth's so unconcerned about her that he accepts the doctor's report."

"You mean then that she's alive at the end of the play?"

"Of course. Macbeth thinks she's died from sleeping sickness, but the truth is that she's run off with the doctor who's responsible for her delicate condition."

The Oxford English Dictionary—
A Negative Note

One day several weeks later when I went into my office, I discovered a number of pages of typed manuscript which had been slipped under the door.

We had recently spent a week discussing Dostoyevsky's *Crime and Punishment*, and Miss LePage had argued that Raskolnikov didn't murder the old pawnbroker and her sister. He had only *imagined* he had done so because he *wanted* to feel guilty. After one of the classes devoted to the novel, Miss LePage asked me if she could write her paper on Dostoyevsky's influence on Philip Roth's *Portnoy's Complaint*.

I had told her it would be better if she limited her paper to *Crime and Punishment,* and she had said, "Well, then, what about a paper on Dostoyevsky's lack of influence on Philip Roth?"

We argued about that for a few minutes, and then she changed the subject by asking what I thought about her transferring her major from business to Jewish Studies.

"Are you Jewish?" I asked her.

"No, of course not—I was born in Iowa—but my boyfriend is, and he says Jewish Studies shouldn't really be for Jews anyway."

I told her that she should take a few courses in any subject before she changed her major.

"I guess I'll stick with business then," she replied, "since it's just about the same thing anyway." Earlier in the week, I had seen her walking across the campus with David Epstein, the student who had dropped my course for Photography. I noticed that Miss LePage was carrying his camera.

When I glanced at the manuscript she had slipped under my office door, I discovered the following note attached to it:

Dear Professor,

After that snide remark you made in class about my not knowing the origins of the word "heavy," I thought I would check it out in the *OED* in the library. About the same time, I discovered that I could get a copy of *The Compact Edition of the Oxford English Dictionary* (complete with magnifying glass) if I joined a certain book club. Which I did. Here's my reaction to the dictionary.

Clara

I must confess, I can't understand why people are so excited about the *Oxford English Dictionary*. After studying the new two-volume edition, I can say categorically that I wish the cepous thing had never been issued in a bifidated edition. The gigantine duodenary edition was less likely to end up as a book club come-on. Now that every seggar can afford a copy, everyone will become a dictionarian. Even worse, I have an ugglesome feeling that Oxford University Press will one day publish a one-volume, paper-backed edition (complete with microscope for easy reading) and every damn swad will own a copy. This isn't just whigmaleery on my part.

I can't understand all the praise that has been heaped on the *OED*. Surely, as a dictionary, the *OED* has a glaring number of errors and omissions. There are, for example, no illustrations, and in a dictionary which refers to cuckoo-flies, potoroos, smerles, porcines, and other strange and mysterious creatures, an occasional illustration would be helpful. The dictionary's description of the sauba is totally inadequate. I have never seen a sauba (so far as I know), and certainly if I ever do, I doubt if I'll recognize it—thanks to the *OED*. Instead of illustrations, there are just words, words, words and plenty of them, except for the important ones the editors omitted. (The same ones which are missing from all the other dictionaries I've ever seen.) I'm not very impressed by editors who take such great pains to go back to Anglo-Saxon to document the origins of many a word and at the same time omit some of our most common expletives. I mean, really, the *OED* would be totally useless if the user were reading Henry Miller or John Updike or just about any other contemporary writer. Now what's the point in compiling the most complete of all dictionaries and then still leaving *those words* out? (Tetra-grammatic words, in case you don't know what I'm referring to, Professor.) Phrenetically speaking, I think they made a bad move here.

Another thing about the *OED* is that the dictionary is basically un-American (a word, incidentally, the *OED* says came into our language in 1818). I won't dispute the origins of un-Americanism, but it does seem to me that people have been un-American a lot longer than that. However, when I say the *OED* is un-American, I mean something else: Noah Webster isn't even mentioned in the definition of "webster." Instead, the *OED* claims that a webster is a weaver, of all things; yet, as any American college student knows, a webster is a dictionary. My roommate is always saying, "Webster says blah-blah-blah." So how can the editors of the most honored dictionary in the English language fail to mention the famous American lexicographer in their definition of the word? See what I mean? This is a very weighty matter. Obstupescence on the part of the editors.

Another thing that I find upsetting about the *OED* is the great number of common words the editors have made complex. There are just too many simple words that have confusing definitions that go on for page after page. Who ever heard of taking twelve pages in a dictionary to explain the word "go"? I mean, if you go someplace, you've simply "gone" (which gets only a fraction of a page), or possibly "went," but nothing is that simple in the *OED*. Twelve whole pages to define a word that any six-year-old can explain in half a sentence. If that isn't enough, the *OED* compilers have found another monosyllabic word that they've devoted almost twice as much space to: "set." Twenty-three pages, or roughly 55,000 words, to explain one simple word? Why, that's longer than Erich Segal's *Love Story*, and yet by the time you've spent the evening reading the definition no one has died and there isn't even anything in all those words to shed a tear over. This will never set right. No word is that wlonk.

I just don't understand how a dictionary can sanctify such excesses. There seems to me to be a basic inconsistency in issuing a two-volume, compact edition of the *OED* to try to save space and money and then taking 55,000 words to define "set." Wait until the ecology people hear about this. And speaking of ecology, the definition that the *OED* gives doesn't even approximate the problems this book itself has raised concerning such matters. Clearly this won't do. You have to turn to some other place in the *OED* before the editors even show the least amount of concern for one of our major problems today: pollution. What does the *OED* tell us about pollution? Very little, if anything, that may be said to be relevant, except for a quotation from the *Daily News* for April 25, 1894: "One of the principal difficulties of freeing the river from pollution was that certain persons had prescriptive rights to pass their sewage into the Thames at Staines and some other places." No wonder the river was stained. Another clear case of moral intrepidy. "Ecology" gets defined in about an inch of type; "pollution" gets about two inches, and yet a few pages later the editors devote more than half a page to the "popinjay." The editors have it all wrong. The world is not going to be polluted by the popinjay. But enough of the quodlibets.

What all of this adds up to is that the editors of the *OED* do not speak the same language most of us do. Flipping through the pages for just a couple of minutes illustrates this. You can't find half the words you are accustomed to using in everyday speech. Words like "schmaltz," "kitsch," "shlemiel"—perfectly good words that we use every day—aren't even in the *OED*. Perhaps this is just a matter of an ethnic bias on the editors' part, although I have a feeling that if they were afraid to use these and other words, it was simply a matter of feeling that readers might get smart and start applying them to the dictionary itself. Or its editors.

What they have chosen to include instead are thousands and thousands of words no one has ever heard of, with long, pedantic definitions and then that cute little *Obs.* symbol after you've carefully read the entire definition, indicating that the word became obsolete in 1723 or some such inanity. Take "manteau," for example, which the *OED* tells us was first used in 1671. A manteau is a woman's undergarment or girdle, depending on who's wearing it and when. After giving us an extended definition of the word, the editors throw another closely related word at us: "manteau-maker." Now, any fool can guess that a manteau-maker makes manteaus. Which is what it *was*, because our editors tell us that the word is obsolete, that the last manteau-maker lived in 1795. Now, what kind of poppycock is that? If manteau is not an obsolete word, if women are still wearing these things, then who the devil's making them? (Unless people just keep wearing the old ones.) The *OED* is full of this kind of thing—while really good words don't even get a tenth of this attention. Pure whifflery.

Sadly, I am left to conclude that the *OED* is the biggest ripoff (a word which, naturally, isn't in the dictionary) in recent book publishing. I just don't understand why people (academics) get so excited about the whole thing. If you add to the issue of the dictionary's total irrelevance the problems related to the production of the two-volume edition, it only makes matters worse. The two volumes are way too large to read in any normal fashion, way too heavy. Each volume weighs so much that you can't read it in bed, for example. My roommate, Sue Generis, found it impossible to read in the bathroom because the magnifying glass kept fogging up. The print in the two-volume edition is so small that last week after I'd finally finished reading it, I had to go out and have my eyes examined. The cost: $45.00 for the examination and $99.00 for a new set of contact lenses. (My father was furious.) That's more than the price of the dictionary itself. Added to that, my friends say they no longer understand half the words I'm using. And the *OED* has also become a threat to my friendship with a certain young man. I'm seriously considering packing it up, sending it back, and canceling my membership.

The *OED?* You can have it. It's a pain in the minook. (Don't look that word up!)

Clara LePage

Portrait of Henry James as a Young Lady

"She is certainly the most significant female novelist I have ever read," she stated, "other than George Eliot, of course."

"Who?" I asked, wondering whom she was referring to. It was my literal-minded student, Clara LePage, at it once again with one of her unorthodox interpretations.

"Henry James," she replied.

"Oh." I found myself somewhat at a loss for words—although I shouldn't have been. We had been discussing James's novel, *The Portrait of a Lady,* and I had just expounded on my theory of "physical relativity" in American fiction: novelists are known by the area of the body their works are most frequently concerned with. By application, Ernest Hemingway's novels generally take place below the belt, whereas F. Scott Fitzgerald's writings are essentially above-the-belt affairs. In such a classification, I had placed Henry James's writings above the neck, although Miss LePage had corrected me and said above the nose. Thus, her comment on the feminine qualities of Henry James's prose did not come as a total surprise.

"Did she ever marry?" Miss LePage asked.

"Who?"

"The authoress—Miss James," she replied, carrying her joke a little too far.

"No, he never did," I replied.

"That's exactly what I thought. Do you know that Ms. Spellman teaches this novel in her Women's Lib course?" She was rummaging around in her bookbag, looking for a cigarette, I assumed; but then to my surprise she brought out a banana and placed it on the table in front of her.

"I'm aware of that," I answered, wondering if Miss LePage was considering changing her major to Women's Studies, wondering at the same time what she was going to do with the banana. The week after Thanksgiving vacation, she had asked me what I thought about the Black Studies program. When she left my office, I noticed that a young black man with a huge Afro was waiting for her in the corridor. For a few minutes, I thought she was going to suggest that Henry James was a black writer.

"My lunch," she mumbled, as she began to eat the banana. "I was quite certain James wasn't married. That explains why he has Isabel Archer become an old maid, though—"

"But he doesn't," I interrupted her. "Didn't you read the second volume of the novel? She gets married."

"Only in a manner of speaking. James clearly based his portrait of Isabel Archer on himself, and since he was an old maid himself, that makes it the same thing, because Gilbert Osmond is hardly more than a neuter. I doubt if the two of them ever got into the same bed together." She took another bite of the banana.

"Miss LePage, aren't you just a little too much concerned about the sexual habits of literary characters? It seems to me you said the same thing about Oedipus and Jocasta at the beginning of the semester. At most, you might say that James modeled Isabel's husband on himself. And if Isabel and Gilbert weren't having a certain frequency in their relations, how could she ever have had a child?"

"Well, there are bound to be accidents from time to time. I doubt if Isabel was smart enough to know anything about birth control." And she added, "What I'm saying is that Isabel Archer married Gilbert Osmond mainly because she was interested in someone else. He was merely a means to that end."

"Who?" I asked her, not without realizing that Miss LePage had placed me in a position where I was playing the straight man.

"Pansy," she replied. "James certainly isn't very subtle with his names, is he?"

"Miss LePage," I replied, the tone of my voice slightly raised, "if I understand you correctly, first you suggested that Henry James modeled the portrait of his heroine upon himself, and now you seem to be implying that Isabel isn't really interested in Gilbert Osmond at all, but only marries him so she can get closer to his daughter, Pansy. Wouldn't you admit that all of this is a little farfetched?" I looked at the other students, hoping they would come to my aid, but they sat there faceless—like stone images.

"Well, lesbianism wasn't exactly invented last week," she replied, "though I admit that Pansy probably wasn't even intelligent enough to realize what her name meant."

"Certainly that doesn't have anything to do with it, does it?" I asked her, as much concerned about the banana as I was about her argument. There was something a little unsettling about her nibbling away at a banana while we argued about Henry James's sexual proclivities.

"Perhaps not. The relationship between the two of them may, more accurately, have been sado-masochistic. The first time James brings Pansy into the novel, he says of her—if I may quote from the text—'She was evidently impregnated with the idea of submission, which was due to anyone who took the tone of authority.' Now if that isn't all rather obvious, I certainly don't know what is. For a feminine novelist, James certainly is obsessed with sexual perversions. Why, there are more dykes in this book than in *The Well of Loneliness*."

"Don't you think you're also a little hung up on sexual interpretations in these books we've been reading, Miss LePage? Couldn't you try some other approach just once this semester?"

"I can't be responsible for what an author writes, can I? It's James who put all the lesbians in his book."

"You mean there are other women in the novel who have the same inclinations—Madame Merle, perhaps?"

"No, of course not—then it would be incestuous.

Madame Merle wanted Isabel to become a prostitute—
anything to keep her away from Pansy. She's the one
straight female in the book." Finished eating the
banana, she folded the skin over several times and
placed it back in her bookbag.

I was wondering why I didn't simply end the class
and tell the students to return to their dormitories. Miss
LePage had clearly ruined the book; there was nothing I
could do to try to salvage it. "Well, at least you can't say
that anyone else is lesbian, can you?" I asked her.

"There is someone else," she replied, "though I
admit that it is handled rather delicately. Isabel's
abhorrence of normal sexual relations is pretty obvious.
Every time she meets a man, she turns around and runs
in the opposite direction. That kiss at the end of the novel
certainly doesn't indicate any usual sexual tendencies.
In fact, Isabel seems to get a real thrill only when she's
kissing one of the other women. Why else does she fawn
over Pansy all the time? And James didn't even bother
to hide her feelings for Henrietta Stackpole. It was Henrietta, I think, who was initially responsible for Isabel's
proclivities."

"I just don't see where you're getting all these ideas,
Miss LePage. You're simply pulling things out of the
novel that aren't there. They're not even implied. You
cannot base a literary interpretation on a general over-
view of the book—you have to use the text, dammit.
Henrietta's about as straight as they come."

"Except in regards to Isabel," Miss LePage replied.
"I don't see any way to interpret it but this way. And
don't tell me I haven't analyzed the text. How else are
we supposed to react when James tells us, 'Henrietta
kissed her, as Henrietta usually kissed, as if she were

afraid she should be caught doing it.' That's right in the middle of page 393 of volume two, and that, it seems to me, is the theme of James's whole novel: in a realistic world, two adults ought to be able to have the kind of relationship they want, and they shouldn't have to be ashamed about it. *The Portrait of a Lady* is James's plea for frankness in sexual relationships among consenting adults. James is a pioneer in his attitudes toward homosexuality."

"If I understand you correctly, what you're saying is that Henry James's novel illustrates a few feminine characteristics and, by implication, that James may have been a latent homosexual. But aren't all people supposed to have latent homosexual tendencies, Miss LePage?"

"Unless they're homosexuals—in which case they have latent heterosexual tendencies."

Ibsen's *Ghosts*
and Interdisciplinary Studies

"What I don't understand is the sequence we followed
for all these books this semester. One week it was Sophocles; the next it was Joseph Conrad. There doesn't seem
to be any order to what we've read—or any connection
between the books."

"I'm not so certain that's absolutely necessary with
Great Books, Miss LePage," I replied. "We're supposed
to be able to read them in any order."

It was the last week of the semester, and Clara
LePage was voicing her opinion about the content of the
course. The week before when we had discussed
Chekhov's *The Sea Gull*, she had relied on her business

background again: if Trepleff had been a little more practical and tried to raise birds for profit, instead of killing them, he wouldn't have needed to commit suicide.

"Why, a course called 'Birds and Literature' would have more unity than these books have with each other. One week you could read *The Sea Gull* and "The Owl and the Pussycat," followed by *Robin Hood, The Cardinal, Youngblood Hawke,* and *Moby Duck.* What this course lacks is a common thread relating all the books to one another—perhaps some sort of interdisciplinary approach."

There—she'd got it out. The week before she had told me she was transferring to another school. "Some place where I can work out an interdisciplinary program," she'd added. I told her I thought she could do that here if she used her imagination.

"How would you organize this course, Miss Le Page?" I asked her, relieved to know that this would be our last absurd dialogue.

"I'm not certain, but I think I'd begin by giving it a flashy new title instead of 'Great Books 101.' You've got to admit that that isn't the most exciting title in the catalogue. I'd probably change it to something like 'From Parricide to Infanticide.' "

" 'Parricide to Infanticide'?" I asked her.

"Why not? Then you could keep the books in the same order. You could use *Oedipus* at the beginning as the example of parricide and you could still end up with *Ghosts* to illustrate infanticide, though some of the others in between might have to be replaced."

"I don't think that we've seen any examples of infanticide this semester, Miss LePage, unless you were thinking we should end with *Medea.*"

"What about Oswald and Mrs. Alving?" she asked me.

"What about them?"

"Well, she kills him at the end of the play, doesn't she? She gives him the medicine, so that's infanticide."

"I wouldn't exactly agree that she murders her son, Miss LePage. And you can't say that Oswald is an infant, can you?"

"As far as his age goes, no, but emotionally he's still a baby. It's still a matter of killing one's child—just as she did her husband earlier."

"Miss LePage, we're talking about Ibsen's *Ghosts*—the problem play about outdated social conventions, if I remember correctly."

"Exactly."

"Then where do you get the idea that Mrs. Alving kills her husband and murders her son?" I asked her.

"That's what the title's about. Isn't there a literary convention that you only have a ghost when there's been an element of foul play? Well, if Mr. Alving had died a normal death he wouldn't be hanging around as a ghost, would he? It's quite clear that Mrs. Alving killed him."

"How? When? Where? For whatever reason why?"

"It's all very simple. Mr. Alving discovered that his wife was playing around with other men, that she was a reckless profligate, and once she discovered that he knew this, she poisoned him. After all, she's always referring to him as her 'contaminated man.' It's a matter of identifying the contaminee and the contaminator."

"Miss LePage, this has got to be the craziest interpretation that has ever been made of Ibsen's *Ghosts*. There are no ghosts in this play."

"Then why is it called *Ghosts?*"

"I mean no ghosts appear on stage as they do in, say, *Hamlet*. There aren't any ghost scenes anywhere."

"I'm talking metaphorically, of course. Although Mr. Alving doesn't appear on the stage in a ghost costume, his presence is always felt. Why else is Mrs. Alving trying to disguise the activities of her past?"

"Miss LePage, it's Mr. Alving who was the sexual profligate, not his wife. All she's trying to do is restore the family name by building the orphanage, if you recall."

She lit a cigarette. "I think you've got everything reversed, Professor."

"In what way?"

"Mrs. Alving—a monster of a woman, I must confess—poisons her husband so she can keep the illegitimate child she has by Engstrand. Only her plan doesn't quite work out, because Oswald runs away as soon as he's old enough and can see that his mother is about to corrupt him also. He can't approve of her liberal ideas—sexual freedom, dirty books, et cetera. She's always trying to get him to read pornography."

"Pornography?"

"Pornography—the books that shock the minister when he visits her. Apparently she's got books like *Oedipus*, *The Secret Sharer*, and *The Portrait of a Lady* lying around her living room and—"

"Miss LePage, don't you think you've made your point?"

"Well, you are just about the most gullible person I've ever met. All I'm trying to do is show you that with all these books, you'd have a gold mine if you'd just advertise the course differently. If my mother knew about all the dirty things we've been reading this semester, she'd write—"

"Miss LePage, don't judge a book by your mother," I couldn't resist saying, beginning to realize that I was going to miss her.

"I think I've come up with a good title for this course, Professor."

"What's that?" I asked her, smiling even before she replied.

" 'Pervertimento'! Use that in the catalogue and next fall you won't be able to keep the students away. Especially the music majors—they'll think it's interdisciplinary—erotic music or something."

Or "Gullible's Travels," I thought to myself.

PART TWO

American Literature
(fall/spring)

Dame Van Winkle's Burden

"I just don't see why everyone's so sympathetic toward Rip Van Winkle. Everyone always says it's his wife's fault. But it isn't. Rip's the guilty one. The trouble with Rip Van Winkle is that he's impotent."

She pronounced the word correctly—my eighteen-year-old red-headed coed—not *im·pō'tent* as the other students would have. That was the problem. The burden of my life, Miss LePage. During the third week of August, I had received a frantic air-mailed, special-deliveried letter from her requesting permission to take my course in American Literature. She had decided to come back and not to transfer to another college as she'd told me at the end of the previous semester. Most courses were closed, had been so since advance registration in

43

the spring, and she needed my permission to add my course. Her letter ended, "I promise that I won't say a word in class if you'll just let me in."

So there she was again, taking a second course from me, and she even tried to remain faithful to her promise—for a time. The first three weeks of the semester, she didn't say anything outrageous in class, though I knew that this silence would be short-lived. When I lectured on Cotton Mather, she looked as if it was all she could do to contain herself. When I got to Jonathan Edwards, I thought she might have apoplexy—except that she wasn't old enough.

By the fourth week (Washington Irving and the early romantics) she couldn't contain herself any longer. The day we got to "Rip Van Winkle," I knew that we were back where we'd been the year before.

"Miss LePage," I asked her, "just how long have you been taking psychology?" (At the beginning of the semester, when I signed her registration form, I noticed that she'd also been able to get into a psychology class.)

"Four weeks, but that doesn't have anything to do with this. I read Freud in high school—two years ago."

"Tell me, as briefly as you can, how you came to the conclusion that Rip Van Winkle is impotent."

"Rip Van Winkle is Washington Irving's alter ego. It was Irving's problem too. I've been reading a biography of him; he never married."

"Miss LePage, just because he never married, that doesn't automatically make him impotent, does it?"

There was another silence. She was beginning to gain everyone's attention—especially the boys'. One of them tried to light a cigarette, but he didn't move his eyes from her until the match had burned his finger. "You've got to look at the story in a different light," she began again, rather slowly. I could see that she was groping—she didn't know what to say. She hadn't anticipated my reaction. But then she continued, "All the symbols in the story—it's a very erotic story, you know—they're all about sex. I'm surprised Irving could get it published. I mean, coming so soon after the Puritans and everything."

"You haven't answered my question, Miss LePage. Just because Irving stayed single, that doesn't necessarily make him impotent, does it? I mean, I'm single too, and that—"

"I wouldn't know. You'd be the best judge of that," she answered blandly. I was glad she'd cut me off. I was losing my train of thought. Miss LePage lit a filter cigarette, emitting dainty little puffs of smoke from her mouth. She looked like an oversized kewpie doll. I could tell that she wasn't inhaling, and I was conscious of the smoke in the room. Smoke was grasping at the ceiling, trying to find an escape.

"You won't deny that Rip's afraid of his wife, will you?" she asked me, before I could change the subject.

"No, I said that a little while ago. That's fairly obvious, I should think."

"Don't you see, then?" she continued. "That's where the whole thing starts. She's too demanding. She's always after his body, to put it rather bluntly. That's why he's always trying to get away from her. That's why he goes off to the mountains in the first place. He's afraid of sex."

"This is all becoming absurd, Miss LePage," I said,

watching her exhale a dainty puff of effluent, blue smoke. It looked as if the cigarette were smoking her as much as she was smoking it.

"I don't think so, sir," another female student interjected. "I know exactly what Clara—Miss LePage—means. I feel the same way. Ever since I read the story in high school. I was thinking last night that my high school English teacher had the wrong interpretation. He was a man. You've got the same ideas. If you were a woman, you'd feel differently. The problem's with Rip, not his wife."

There was a noticeable silence. I had hoped that some of the males in the class would come to my rescue, but they didn't. They just sat there stupidly, watching Miss LePage puff away at her cigarette. I had a perverse desire to hear her start coughing, but she didn't.

"I read the story very carefully last night," Miss LePage said, "twice. And I think I know what Irving was trying to say."

"That he was impotent," I said, a little too smugly.

She ignored my comment and went on, "Everything's there—right in the story. All the symbols."

"Such as?" I asked her, beginning to feel hopeless.

"The gun, for example. Rip's gun—it doesn't work. Irving says it's rusty—the barrel is 'encrusted with rust, the lock falling off, and the stock worm-eaten.' That's a quote from the text."

"That's at the end of the story," I told Miss LePage.

"Well, I can't see that it matters much. When he comes down to the village after his sleep, he's still the same. And he's been sleeping for twenty years. That's purely Freudian. Rip Van Winkle's not only impotent—he's an escapist. That's the point—he's avoiding his wife instead of trying to work out his problems with her. The whole sleep is nothing more than an intensely erotic dream. Wishful thinking."

"How can you say that?" I asked, raising my voice a little. "There isn't one thing in the entire story that says what he dreamed about."

"What do you mean? The whole thing in the mountains. It's all a dream. Ninepins and liquor. If that isn't clear, I don't know what is. That's what did it in the first place—too much drink. He was always hanging out at the village inn—even at the end of the story. And all those dirty little men playing with those ninepins—certainly you can see what that means. Talk about—"

"All right, all right. Tell me one thing, Miss LePage. Just how do you explain Rip's marriage in the first place? How do you explain the two children? Illegitimate, I suppose?" I thought I heard a snigger from the class.

"I'm not certain," Miss LePage replied. "They could be. Dame Van Winkle was known to be playing around with peddlers—but I don't think that's what Irving meant. At least not until later. I think they're probably Rip's. Irving says, 'Times grew worse and worse with Rip Van Winkle as years of matrimony rolled on.' I think that's pretty obvious. He was all right at the beginning when they were first married, but then it got worse—it was too much drink. Shakespeare says the same thing in *Macbeth*. The Porter—"

"I know, I know," I interrupted, not certain whether I should be happy that she remembered something we read the year before or chastise her. The whole thing was really going too far. The smoke in the room was making it almost impossible to breathe. I was afraid I was going to start choking.

But she continued, "Rip's dog, Wolf, for example. He's really a symbol of everything Rip should be. You'll notice at the end of the story he barks at Rip—mocks him, actually. It's Dame Van Winkle whom Wolf's been staying with all those years. And Dame Van Winkle, I don't see how you can feel anything for her but sympathy. Rip drives her to the streets."

"Drives her to the streets? Where'd you get that?" I asked her, feeling the stagnant air in my lungs about to explode.

"At the end of the story. The last thing Irving says about her—if I may quote it—is 'She broke a blood vessel in a fit of passion at a New England peddler.' And they weren't arguing. At least not over *his* price. That would be too obvious."

Poe's Raven—The Last Word

"I think Griswold did the right thing," she commented. "It was either distort Poe's image or tell the truth and ruin his reputation forever."

It was Clara LePage, referring to Edgar Allan Poe's literary executor, the infamous Reverend Rufus W. Griswold. Critical consensus holds that Griswold is responsible for many of the erroneous myths surrounding Poe's life. Miss LePage, however, as I was beginning to learn, usually held an opinion contrary to the critics'. The week before, after complaining that American writers gave an unfair picture of women (no great discovery on her part), she had suddenly argued that Cooper's Natty Bumppo was really a woman in disguise. (A frontiersman in drag was the way she had put it.)

"So you think Griswold did the right thing by start-
ing the myth of Poe as a drunkard and a dope fiend? You
know, Miss LePage, you're probably the only person
currently living who hasn't criticized Griswold for what
he did." I glanced around at the other twenty-four students in the class. They appeared, however, to be taking
little interest in the discussion, except for one student
who was fiddling with a tape recorder.

"It was better to distort Poe's image than tell the
truth—at least for a reading audience as puritanical as
Poe's."

"You've lost me, Miss LePage," I replied, already
annoyed at her interpretation without even hearing it.
"But let's get it out, so we can go on to his short stories."

"It's very simple, Professor. Poe didn't die from
alcohol or even drugs. He died from syphilis, so it's
perfectly logical that—"

"Syphilis, Miss LePage?" I interrupted. "How in
the world did you come up with that?"

"It's right here in 'The Raven.' The clue's been
there for years, just waiting for someone to interpret it
the way Poe intended. I don't understand how critics can
be so obtuse. What else do you think the Raven keeps
telling him?"

"Surely not that he's got syphilis," I told her, the
pitch of my voice clearly belying my more than startled
concern.

"No, not that exactly, but a reminder that he's got it
and can't get rid of it, if you see what I mean."

"Well, frankly, I don't, Miss LePage. Would you
mind giving me a hint or two?"

I watched her stall for time, certain for once that I'd

50

backed her into a corner. She removed a cigarette from her package on the table, lit it, and took a more than dainty puff—all the time smiling ever so coyly in my direction. The rest of the students looked on as if Miss LePage were the one who would tell them the true account of Poe's stormy literary career. The student with the tape recorder pushed the button as she began.

"Well, I've read the poem very carefully, and it seems to me that this is the only valid interpretation."

"Go on, Miss LePage."

"One night when Poe is sitting in his study, reading a book—"

"How do you know it's Poe and not someone else?" I asked her, certain that I had caught her even before she had the chance to get to "The Raven." "How can you assume that the person in a literary work is the author?"

"You told us yourself that Poe's poems are highly autobiographical. Anyway, the clues are obvious."

"All right, go on."

"Well, anyway, Poe's sitting there reading a medical dictionary in his study."

"Look, Miss LePage, you know there's nothing in the poem that says he's reading a medical dictionary."

"You're wrong, Professor. That's how it all relates to 'The Raven,' don't you see? Poe's reading a medical dictionary to see if he can find a cure for his disease. And that's why he welcomes the Raven, a bird of good omen—just in case the bird happens to know of a cure. If I may quote from the text, Poe asks the Raven,

> . . . *tell me truly, I implore:*
> *Is there—is there balm in Gilead?—tell me—*
> *tell me, I implore!*

51

He thinks that the Raven may know of a cure—of some medicinal herb which will cure him of the disease."

"But you haven't proven that he's got a disease, Miss LePage, let alone that the Raven is something to be welcomed because of its medical knowledge. The next thing you'll be saying is that the Raven attended Harvard Medical School." I was almost at my wits' end.

She ignored my comment. "He's got all the symptoms. Can't sleep, a cold sweat, a burning bosom—as he says, 'my soul within me burning'—clear indications that his case is more than a slight one. After all, it was 1845—just four years before Poe died. And he's been trying all those drugs and they don't work. Remember, Professor, this was before the age of penicillin. Why else do you think he sits around taking all those shots of nepenthe?"

"I give up, Miss LePage. You've already refuted a hundred years of literary scholarship which says that the bird is an evil omen."

"That's not so. Poe welcomes him, thinking he's got a cure. The clues are obvious. If you remember, Poe tells the Raven to sit on a bust of Pallas. Because of the censors, he had to cover things up a bit. What he really meant was a statue of a phallus."

I could feel the blood rush to my face; I realized that the students knew I was blushing. "Miss LePage, I really do think you're going too far."

"No, let me finish. Poe thinks the Raven is going to help him find the cure. But instead, the bird turns out to be his conscience—a reminder that never again will he enjoy those nights of sexual promiscuity. That's why the bird keeps repeating 'Nevermore.' "

What could I say? At this stage I didn't care if I ever

read the damn poem again. But I felt obliged to salvage the interpretation for the benefit of the other students.

"There's just one thing that worries me about your interpretation, Miss LePage. You've forgotten something—one of the most important elements of the poem."

"What's that?" She extinguished her cigarette in an ash tray and glanced, momentarily, at the other students.

"Lenore—the woman in the poem. The woman Poe says he loves. What's she got to do with all this? I suppose Poe gave her the disease also?"

"No, you've got it all wrong. She gave it to him. That's why he hates women so much."

Strange Goings On at Walden Pond

"You haven't convinced me that there's very much to admire about Henry David Thoreau," she said.

It was coming to the time when I began to dread meeting my American Literature students. Miss LePage was beginning to dominate my entire consciousness. At night, when I tried to get to sleep, she was on my mind—as I lay there in bed for hours, trying to guess what she'd say in the next class. If I slept, she even entered into my dreams, giving me no peace at all. Lately, I'd had the feeling that Clara LePage was my Raven, telling me, "Nevermore—you'll never be able to teach a class without me—nevermore."

"Can't you admire Thoreau for living alone in the

woods for two years?" I asked her, hoping that for once she would let matters stay as they were.

"I think it's a complete fraud."

"What?" I asked her, not certain if she meant the two years or the book itself.

"*Walden*," Miss LePage replied. "It certainly must be one of the most hypocritical works ever published. Such vanity—and to think that for years critics have been echoing all that praise."

"I don't believe I understand what you're getting at, Miss LePage."

"Isolation—living alone at the pond—the critics swallowed that whole myth. All I can say is that their arithmetic is pretty poor. Why, all you have to do is add a few things together and you can see that Thoreau was hardly out at the pond at all. It's all right there in the book, too. That's why I can't see how everyone gets so excited about Thoreau's staying out in the woods."

"I think you've lost me, Miss LePage," I told her. "I'm not at all certain what you're trying to say. If the book isn't a study in isolation, then what is it?"

"Gregariousness," she replied, almost before I had finished talking. "Thoreau's most gregarious years were the two he spent at Walden Pond. Oh, sure, he was out there in the woods—a few miles from town, but he had more visitors during those two years at Walden than at any other time in his life. That is, when he was out there. Most of the time he was running back into Concord to see if anything had happened in the few hours he'd been away."

"I don't see how you can say that, Miss LePage."

"It's right in the book—there's textual evidence. He tells us that once every day or at least every other day he went into Concord. And if he wasn't there, he was always bothering the people at Baker Farm. By my calculation, Thoreau was at the pond no more than one-third of the time—mostly to sleep there. Once he even says he was away from the pond for two weeks. It's obvious that he hated the place and that he'd do anything he could to stay in town. You'll notice that he even says, 'I have traveled a good deal in Concord,' admitting that he's not been staying out at the pond."

"Miss LePage, don't you think that all this is a little irrational—in light of what Thoreau says about his night in the Concord jail?"

"That's just it. Don't you see? He had to bribe Emerson so he wouldn't bail him out—anything so he could stay a night in Concord."

"—?"

I looked out the window, wondering if there was anything I could do to save Thoreau's masterpiece. I had spent the first half-hour of the class expounding on the virtues of solitary living, and now Miss LePage had negated almost everything I had said. "Well, that's a very unusual interpretation, Miss LePage, but hardly one that can be supported by the book."

"I don't see why not," she replied. "Everything I've said is right in the book. Thoreau's the one who says he's traveled a lot in Concord. That's not my line. It's perfectly clear that he kept going into town so he could sponge a good meal off someone. He must have bummed so many meals those years that the townspeople could hardly wait to see him move away from Walden and get an honest job. After all, about all he had out at the pond were beans, and he was busy using them for something else."

"What do you mean, Miss LePage?" I asked her, hoping that I could illustrate the flaws in her logic.

"Well, I'm not trying to suggest that he was another George Washington Carver or anything like that, but you know as well as I do, Professor, that no one could eat that many bushels of beans. Not even Henry David Thoreau. He was doing something else with them."

"What was that, Miss LePage?" I was almost afraid to ask her.

"Well, he almost makes a fetish out of the pure Walden pond water—except when he pollutes it by bathing in it every morning. I think he was doing something with the water from the pond and the beans. And all that molasses. There are just too many references to the pits he'd dug under the house and the big crocks there. I think he was probably trying to distill some liquor out of the beans—or ferment them into brandy or something. Why else would he spend all that time cultivating all those rows of beans?"

"Bean brandy, Miss LePage? Thoreau was an avowed teetotaler. No one ever saw him touch a drop of drink in his life."

"I know that, but that doesn't stop him from selling it to others, does it?"

I stood there with my hands on the sides of my head, knowing too well that there was nothing I could do to get her to change her interpretation.

"That's what bothers me most about him," she said.

"What, Miss LePage?"

"His obsession with economy—always making a profit. Everytime you turn a page there's another column of figures, and Thoreau's telling you how much money he's saved. He's worse than Ben Franklin that way. If he were living today, he'd be an economist working for the government."

"Miss LePage, does this really have anything to do with *Walden?*"

"Well, sort of. My point is that Thoreau was making money the whole time he was out at Walden Pond. I'll bet he even sold his house for a profit when he left. Remember, he says at one place, 'I enhanced the value of the land by squatting on it.' Now if that doesn't illustrate an obsession with making a fast buck, I don't know what does."

"Is there anything else you want to say, Miss Le Page, now that you've ruined the whole book for us?"

"Well, if you have to put it that way, just one more thing."

"What's that?"

"I think there was someone living with him all the time he was out at Walden Pond."

"Who? Margaret Fuller?" I couldn't resist asking.

"No—an Indian. An Indian woman."

"Oh, come on—this is crazy!" I was weary of the whole thing.

"That's what the title means—*Walden.* It's an Indian name, as he tells us. Thoreau had an Indian squaw he kept out there at his cabin. That's how he made his biggest profit. There was a lot more hanky-panky going on out at Walden Pond than people have suspected."

"How do you know that, Miss LePage?"

"It's right in the book. Thoreau says, 'I have had twenty-five or thirty souls, with their bodies, at once under my roof.' Now if that isn't a strange way of putting it, I certainly don't know what is. Why that poor Indian woman—"

AMERICAN LITERATURE (FALL/SPRING)

But the bell rang, and we will never know what Miss LePage's true sympathies for the Indian woman were.

Hester Prynne and the Pill

Sometime after five-thirty, after being awakened a third time by the beating of the bird's wings against his window, he crawled out of bed, put on his glasses, and searched in the dark for his undershorts. Once found, he pulled them up his skinny white legs and buttoned the snaps while groping his way through the bedroom and down the hall into the kitchen, through the darkness to the back door. He stood there for a minute, trying to construct the best plan of action, wondering mostly what would be the best thing to throw at the ugglesome creature. Then, suddenly afraid that it would be bigger than he, he stood there trembling, listening for any noise that might be coming from the other side of the door. He stood there, it seemed, for hours, until he finally got hold of his nerves and unlocked the door. There was nothing there, of course. The bird had vanished, so he slowly walked outside (barefoot) into the damp grass of the backyard, still contemplating the safest course of action. Then he realized—the bird was still at his bedroom window.

In the flower garden, or, rather, *around* the flower garden he had so painstakingly cleaned out the month before, pieces of white quartz glistened in the early morning dew. He bent over, still not quite awake, almost losing his balance, but managing to grasp several of the smaller pieces in his left hand. Quartz in readiness, he stood up and edged his way to the corner of the house; he rubbed his eyes under his glasses with his free hand, trying to focus on the blackness in the backyard as he nosed his face around the corner. But the bird was not there. Or if it was, he couldn't see it; and he realized it had been frightened by the sound of the door being opened. He stood there, transplanted against the building like the malignant tumor of a tree jutting out in some unorthodox position, wondering if he would ever be free of the frustration of the bird's nightly vigil. Then, when he was about to return to the house, he detected the slightest movement in the distance near the garbage cans, not so far from the garden.

But it wasn't the raven. It was a tomcat, and in that moment when the animal realized that it was being hunted, he hurled all three of the stones in his hand toward it, scattered fashion; each one missed the mark by half a dozen feet. As the cat bounded off toward the bushes in the neighbor's yard and up into the safety of a tree, he, distraught, headed back toward the door, realizing that the bird/cat had won once again, as it had been winning every night of the past week, and that he had only to go back to bed and fall asleep so that the mysterious creature could again awaken him with its incessant "Nevermore," like the voices of his students in the recent demonstrations.

He had never been a good shot.

When he got back to his bedroom, he was surprised to find his American Literature students waiting for him, sitting on his bed.

"Hester's problem is that she thinks she's frigid," Miss LePage began, looking at the other students for support. He noticed then that only his female students were sitting on his bed.

"She's what?" he asked, bleary-eyed from the lack of sleep, wondering if, in truth, he had heard her comment correctly. The day before, when he had grabbed a cup of coffee at the student union, he had noticed her manning the booth run by the Women's Liberation girlies, wondering why petite Miss LePage, of all his students, would take an interest in their movement. (Weeks before, at the same booth, he had overheard a rather masculine-looking girl say to another, "Sometimes I feel as if I really do have a penis." Her image had remained in his mind, and he had come to associate the Women's Liberation movement with large, unattractive young women.)

Then she continued, moving back a little on his bed, almost sitting on his pillow, "She's frigid—or so she thinks—and afraid that she's not supposed to enjoy sex. The whole novel is nothing but a plea for more enjoyable sexual relations and Hester's realization that the *A* on her breast doesn't mean 'awful' or something dirty at all, but *amour,* ardor—love!"

He lit a cigarette, pondering her interpretation, thinking it really wasn't so bad after all, albeit a little oversimplified. "Was she French?" he asked her. But he continued before she could answer his question, "What's to prevent her from making that discovery right away?"

"Well, the men certainly don't help the situation very much," she replied, "—helpless creatures that they are." She looked at the other women on his bed, and they nodded their heads in agreement.

"I supposed you'd say that," he continued, the image of Miss LePage at the Women's Liberation booth returning to his mind. "I'm rather surprised you didn't call them dirty old men." He was suddenly aware that his students had noticed that all he was wearing was his undershorts.

"Well, of course, that's taken for granted. Dirty may be putting it rather mildly. Hester didn't care much for their idea of a *mélange à trois*. Perhaps in a way her frigidity was to her advantage, since she'd certainly have run amuck if she'd gotten to the point where she really enjoyed sex. I guess I'd be frigid, too, with Chillingworth and Arthur Dimwit always putting their hands on me."

"I think you're contradicting yourself, Miss Le Page," he remarked, wondering how he could change the subject, wondering how he was ever going to get these women out of his bedroom. He stood there, hands over his groin, trying to act as nonchalant as possible.

"All I said was that Hester Prynne was essentially a frigid woman and that Arthur Dimmesdale was a sex fiend who took advantage of a good thing when he saw it—of a young woman who'd never known a moment's peace from the men around her. Why do you suppose she ran off to America in the first place?"

"I was under the general impression that her husband sent her there. Was there another reason?"

Miss LePage looked at him as if he hadn't read the novel in question, and then said, a little too calmly, "You surely don't believe that, do you? Hester ran away from her husband because he denied her any human rights at all. How ironic, of course, that once she gets to Salem she runs into someone even worse. Chillingworth at least had some sort of backbone in him; Dimmesdale was nothing more than an oversexed minister, the kind you always found in the colonies. Hester was the real pillar of support."

"Would you say that Hester believes she has a penis?" he asked before he realized what he was saying. He was afraid the women on his bed would make faces at him, but they made no reaction to what he'd said.

"I don't think we have to go that far," she replied, skillfully turning the tables, "though I suppose you could say that Hester does realize that in Puritan New England a woman hasn't got a chance at all."

"I don't quite follow your train of thought," he replied, closing his eyes, thinking that she might disappear. But when he opened them, all that had happened was that his bedroom had changed to the classroom, though he was still standing there—in front of all those women—clad only in his shorts.

"Essentially, it's a very simple situation," Miss LePage continued. "If Hester were living today, she wouldn't have to go through all that humiliation. There's the pill, and you can be damn certain that Hester's got enough sense not to want half a dozen brats squalling around her. One Pearl is enough."

"But that's hardly the point—we're not dealing with

a treatise on birth control, Miss LePage. We're dealing with a piece of literature, and you can't simply say that Hester Prynne would have been all right if she'd been on the pill. A little less neurotic, perhaps, but—"

"Neurotic?" Miss LePage interrupted. "Are you talking about Hester or the men? Hester's a pillar of stability in a nightmare of confusion. She's certainly not the one who's cracking up at the end of the story. You men—you always put the blame on women. Wait until there's a pill for men, and then you'll see what it's like."

"I think you're getting a little removed from the subject, Miss LePage." He was beginning to lose his cool. He thought about the cat/bird crying at his back window and wished he were back in his bed. Why did he have to keep having these inane conversations?

Then she continued, "You certainly don't think *The Scarlet Letter* is very flattering toward women, do you? If Margaret Fuller had written it, I can assure you things would have ended differently."

"If, if, if—" he interrupted, sputtering noticeably in front of the women in the classroom. Tiny beads of perspiration had broken out all over his nose. He looked outside the classroom, thinking that he could see the wings of a large, black bird beating at the window. In a flash the image changed to the branches of a tree. "Literature deals with possibilities and only at times with realities, Miss Le Page," he said, but as soon as he made the statement he wondered if he hadn't meant the opposite of what he'd said. Then he continued, "Let's face it, Hester Prynne got pregnant, and in those days there wasn't much she could do about it. It doesn't change anything saying she should have been on the pill."

"She could have led the masses if she hadn't had all

those horny men around her." For a moment it seemed as if Miss LePage were finished, but she continued, "I wonder if I might ask you a question?"

"Of course," he replied, hoping he could bring the dialogue to a conclusion.

"What killed Dimmesdale and Chillingworth?"

"Guilt, of course—they finally realized they were responsible for the way they treated Hester." The answer had popped out, without his even having to think about it.

"That's exactly what I thought you'd say. You men are all alike—trying to make us believe that you accept the responsibility for our subjugation."

"You've got another interpretation?" he asked her.

"If you'd care to know," she replied—a little too smug, he thought, again looking at the other girls for support.

"Yes, of course, what killed them off?"

"Syphilis."

"Syphilis—who'd they get it from, Edgar Allan Poe?" There, surely that would outfox her.

"I'm serious. And if you'll turn to page 192 of the text you'll see that Dimmesdale says, if I may quote it for you, 'Methought the germ of it was dead in me.' "

"So what's your argument, Miss LePage?"

"It's obvious, don't you see? Dimmesdale's guilt is that he believes he's given Hester the clap, while in truth it was the other way around. Hester, who got it from Chillingworth in the first place, gave it to Dimmesdale, and he's so simple he's afraid to ask Hester if she's got it too."

"I suppose that's why Dimmesdale's always scratching his chest," he commented, again surprised at what he'd said. But there was no response from the girls; they might just as well not even have been there.

"Hester, of course, has it too—since she gave it to Dimmesdale—but it doesn't kill her like the others. She's only a carrier—she's too strong—it's only the men who can't get rid of it. Why do you think Chillingworth spends all his time searching around in the woods, if it isn't for a cure—"

It was beginning to be a little too much for him. He was aware that Miss LePage was slowly changing into a tomcat, crying out in the night. He was afraid to ask her the most obvious question of all, yet he knew he would never escape until he asked it, that she would sit there purring until he asked her.

"And the A—what does it stand for?"

"Abortion. What else? You don't suppose she gave a damn that it was adultery, do you?"

The word quickly spread around the campus. One of the professors in the English department had climbed a tree. Climbed right out of the classroom window into the security of the leaves of an oak tree where he remained, trembling for the duration of the day, as the girls in the Women's Liberation movement marched around the trunk—voices and placards rising toward the sky:

"Super Orgasm."

"Don't Make Babies or War—Nevermore."

"The Pill Isn't Enough."

And Miss LePage's private truth: "Hester Prynne Didn't Have a Chance. Will You?"

Moby Dick and Sexless Politics

"I'm afraid," Miss LePage said, "that you've over-looked the most important aspect of Melville's novel."

I was surprised at her comment, because I didn't think she was paying any attention. For the past ten minutes, she had been filing her fingernails—a sharp, grating noise whenever I stopped talking—and the sound was beginning to drive me crazy. Wouldn't she ever stop? Her comment momentarily reduced me to a state of incoherence, but then I realized that if I got her involved in the discussion, she might stop her annoying activity.

"What do you mean, Miss LePage?" I managed to question, groping for the support of the lectern. The fingernail file was still going twenty miles an hour.

"The political implications."

"Oh, really? Would you mind explaining yourself a little?" We were discussing *Moby Dick,* and I must confess I was relieved that for once she appeared to have forgotten sex.

"Isn't the mark of a great piece of literature its efficaciousness for later generations?" she asked, parodying, I knew, what I had said in more than one class during the semester. She stopped filing her nails, and I watched her open her purse and dig around for something else.

"Yes, of course," I replied rather slowly, wondering what she was going to do next.

"Well, then, it's all there," she said, still rummaging around in her purse with one hand and pointing at her copy of *Moby Dick* with the other. "You hardly even have to look for it." She pulled a bottle of nail polish out of her purse, twisted the cap, and began to paint her nails—tangerine orange, or some horrible color like that. I thought I detected laughter from someone in the class, but I wasn't certain if it was because of her statement or because of what she was doing.

"Would you mind giving me just a little clue?" I asked her, wondering how she could paint her nails and talk at the same time.

"All I'm saying is that Melville has set up a very political situation in *Moby Dick,* rooted in our basic sexual differences. After all, there's a very good possibility that it's a female whale, you know."

"Miss LePage, don't you ever tire of these sexual interpretations? Do you have to read Women's Lib into every book we read in this course? Moby Dick is a female whale. Hester Prynne should have been on the pill. Where do you get these lame-brained ideas? Don't you think—"

"I don't know what you're talking about."

"Last week you said that Hester Prynne could have been a leader of a women's movement if she'd only been on the pill."

"I wasn't even in class last week, Professor. I missed the entire week." She continued painting her nails.

I looked at the other students, hoping they would help clarify the matter. "Is that right?" I finally asked one of them.

But another one replied, "She's right, Prof, she's been gone the last three classes."

"Are you kidding me?" I asked them, beginning to wonder if I were losing my mind.

"I thought you'd at least miss me," Miss LePage continued. "I wanted to tell you about this theory I have about the *A* on Hester's breast, but—"

"Never mind. Let's just stick to *Moby Dick*, all right? But stop dickering around with the text."

"Well, I think that Melville's novel is a perfect example of what Kate Millett was trying to say in *Sexual Politics*." She had finished painting her left hand and was waving it in the air so it would dry.

"What are you talking about, Miss LePage?"

"The dynamics of power in heterosexual relationships. As I see it, the political parties in the United States are rooted in basic sexual roles, and the implications of these roles are boundless. The Republican party is masculine (or at least professes to be so); the Democratic party is feminine. And the struggle between the two of them is symbolic of the basic male/female relationship. Without this obvious sexual origin of our two political

70

parties, the whole system would collapse. This is the real meaning of 'sexual politics.' "

"Ah, would you mind explaining this a little more thoroughly?"

She began painting the nails on her right hand. "I've worked it all out. Everything that the two parties stand for relates back to sex—politics is little more than the battle of the sexes. Ms. Millett simply didn't understand her thesis. Republicans are conservative, typified by big business and utilitarianism. Their beliefs are all based on attempts to increase their masculinity, so they call out for law and order, they always bring up the threat of Communism, and so on. It's the Republicans who keep the wars going. They always try to cultivate the big, tough image of strength and dominance. As a party, they associate themselves with all the things that are assumed to represent masculinity."

"And the Democrats?" I asked her.

"The opposite—femininity. The Democrats are the doves in any war, and in Republican eyes all Democrats are too liberal, too soft on Communism, always willing to compromise—passive, in so many words, just like women are supposed to be. The irony of all this is that the Republican party—in its attempts to appear supermasculine—turns out to be the party of sexual inadequacy. You don't ever hear of any Republican involved in a sex scandal, do you?" She waved her right hand in the air so the nails would dry.

"But Kate Millett's book wasn't trying to do anything like this, Miss LePage. And what's this got to do with *Moby Dick* anyway?"

"Well, if Ms. Millett had understood the true impli-

71

cations of sex in politics, she could have applied her theories to all these sexless books we've been reading this semester."

"What do you mean, Miss LePage?" I was aware that I had almost called her Ms. LePage.

"Emerson and Thoreau—softies from way back, against war, so they were obviously feminine—Democrats."

"Miss LePage, don't you think you've carried this idea just a bit too far?"

"All these books are political, Professor. The system is infallible; it can be applied to all works of literature."

"Suppose you give us one more example," I replied, thinking I could catch her at her own system.

"Well, *The Scarlet Letter,* for example. Hester's a Democrat and Arthur Dimmesdale's a Republican. After all, it's rather obvious who seduced whom. Or *Moby Dick.* Ahab's a Republican (an authority figure) and the whale's a Democrat."

It was beginning to go too far, but she continued before I could cut her off. "If you want to use something more recent, look at *Portnoy's Complaint.* Alexander Portnoy's clearly a Democrat and Sophie Portnoy, his mother, is a Republican. Don't you see?" she asked, as she finally stopped talking.

"Just another question, Miss LePage. Under this system, how would you classify someone like Norman Mailer—Republican or Democrat?"

"Republican—what else—like most twentieth-century American writers who are hung up about masculinity: Hemingway, Fitzgerald, Wolfe—the whole damn lot of them."

AMERICAN LITERATURE (FALL/SPRING)

"And Kate Millett herself?" I asked.
"Republican also. It's all rather obvious, isn't it?"

Leaves of Grass—Pure Acapulco Gold

"**W**as Walt Whitman flying when he wrote *Leaves of Grass?*"

It was January. The second half of American Literature: Walt Whitman to Allen Ginsberg. God only knew what I could expect from Miss LePage. At the end of the previous semester, she'd flown off to Aspen, Colorado, for Christmas vacation and a month of skiing, informing me before she left that she definitely had given up the idea of majoring in business. Her interests had become more diversified—"something interdisciplinary" she'd mumbled as she handed in her blue book at the end of the exam. "But I'll take the rest of American Lit—don't you worry," she said, fleeing out of the room before I had the chance to say good-bye. "I've got to catch my plane."

Her question about Whitman wasn't exactly unexpected, though I had thought she wasn't paying any attention. She had been knitting during the entire period—an indistinguishable object of reds and browns, and I had stood there, behind the lectern, noticeably annoyed, wondering how I could get her to stop.

"Just exactly what do you mean, Miss LePage?"

"Was Whitman high when he wrote *Leaves of Grass?*"

"I've never thought about it that way," I replied, "but I don't think so." I looked at some of the other students, expecting that the subject would be dropped and we could return to the discussion topic I had introduced: the Freudian overtones of Whitman's poetry.

Miss LePage began again, still knitting, "It seems to me that the poems in *Leaves of Grass* are nothing but a plea on Whitman's part for a more mature attitude toward drug usage in this country."

I looked at her, wondering how she could continue her knitting and concentrate on the discussion at the same time. How was I supposed to answer a question like that, anyway?

"Now, really, Miss LePage, the grass in Whitman's title applies to something entirely different from what we think of as grass today. It's just plain, ordinary grass like—"

"Then it's obvious that you haven't examined the poems very carefully," she said, the knitting needles continuing at their same rhythmic speed. I wasn't certain what I could do to turn the discussion back to Freud. Then Miss LePage continued, "There are simply too many references to the whole drug culture to make them appear accidental; and I'm not referring to metaphoric references, Professor, but the outright references to drugs scattered throughout many of the poems."

"Such as?" I asked, leaning on the lectern, looking for some clue in the faces of the other students. A young man in the back row lit a cigarette, and I was certain I identified an aroma I had not detected in the classroom earlier. The effrontery that some students exhibit these days never ceases to amaze me. Talk about pot and they light up a joint. It gets so that I'm almost afraid to mention sex in class.

"The most obvious references are to grass itself, which certainly meant the same thing a hundred years ago as it does today. But Whitman talks about other things too. The second section of 'Song of Myself' describes a fragrance in the air—rooms full of perfumes— and right after that Indians smoking a peace pipe, though I admit it's highly unlikely that that's what they're smoking. There's more obvious proof in the first line of the fourth stanza, where he begins, 'Trippers and askers surround me. . .' " She had momentarily stopped her knitting so she could consult the text of the poem. "That is about as blatant as it could be. If there is one thing that's wrong with Whitman's approach, it's his directness. He's anything but subtle."

I was about to tell her that "trippers" probably meant something different in Whitman's day—that she should check the word in the *OED*—but thought better about making that suggestion. She continued, "The fifteenth section contains a direct reference to an opium eater, and the ensuing passages contain a plethora of symbolic references relating to journeys and trips. For example, Whitman says, 'I believe a leaf of grass is no less than the journey-work of the stars,' injecting a mystical overtone into the poem."

"Miss LePage, even if 'grass' and 'journey' meant the same thing to Whitman as they do to you, that doesn't necessarily mean that Whitman's suggesting that everyone else has to smoke pot, does it?"

She had resumed her knitting. "Not entirely, of course; but when Whitman talks of other drugs, too, I don't see how you can possibly negate the fact that, as he says in section twenty-four," and she again consulted the text, " 'I will accept nothing which all cannot have their counterpart of on the same terms.' "

"He's talking about democracy," I told her.

"All the more reason for relaxing the restrictions on pot," she said, glancing for a minute at the row of stitches she had just completed. Then she continued, "In the thirty-third section he talks about acid and speed."

That was going too far. She simply had to be stopped. "Miss LePage, this interpretation doesn't make any sense at all. How can you talk of acid and speed when the drugs didn't even exist in Whitman's time?"

"Neither did Freud, but that certainly didn't prevent you from going into a Freudian analysis of the poem."

"It's not the same thing at all"—raising my voice to a more noticeable pitch. I wanted to walk over to her and yank the knitting out of her hands, but I worked at retaining my cool.

"Why not? It seems to me that it's just as valid to talk about mind-expanding drugs in *Leaves of Grass* as to—"

"Where? Show me where"—barely restraining myself from shouting. "Where in the poem does Whitman talk about acid and speed?"

Dropping her knitting again, she opened her book, but not until she had looked at the rest of the students. "Stanza thirty-three, the longest section of the poem, is nothing but an extended description of Whitman's turning on. It's pure psychedelia. I'm surprised the poem wasn't banned when it was published."

"It was," I told her, "but for other reasons." Which I certainly was not going to go into.

"Oh." But she continued. "You will notice at the beginning, just as he's turning on he says, 'Space and Time! now I see it is true, what I guess'd at. /What I guess'd when I loaf'd on the grass . . .' "

"That's not acid and speed—" I told her.

"How do you know?"

"A—a—if you're asking—"

"I'll show you. Just a little later. He's still just using his nickel bag. As he begins to get a little high, he talks of floating and uses the word itself; and then he switches to the other drugs, recording his trip in detail:

> *Speeding through space, speeding through heaven and the stars,*
> *Speeding amid the seven satellites and the broad ring, and the diameter of eighty thousand miles,*
> *Speeding with tail'd meteors, throwing fire-balls like the rest. . . .*

And he continues, with a clear reference to the fact that he's now on something else, 'I fly those flights of a fluid and swallowing soul.' Three lines later Whitman shows how stupid it is to have so many laws against dope. He says, 'No guard can shut me off, no law prevent me.' "

AMERICAN LITERATURE (FALL/SPRING)

She stopped and glanced up from her text as if she were expecting my approval of her interpretation. But I knew the poem too well. "Exactly how do you interpret the next few lines, Miss LePage, when Whitman says, continuing the same fluid imagery, 'All this I swallow, it tastes good, I like it well, it becomes mine, / I am the man, I suffer'd, I was there'? Is he drinking booze now?"

"A bad trip," she answered, without even having to think about it, her knitting needles once again flying at full speed. "He's simply had too much—or bad stuff. Whitman isn't trying to hide the side effects—that's what's so good about him. Each man should be free to have this kind of experience—if he wants it. It relates to his whole theory of *Democratic Vistas*. He makes this clear a little later when he says, 'Not I, not any one else can travel that road for you, / You must travel it for yourself.' "

I had a sudden revelation: the only way to stop her was to play her own game—but to play it better than she. "Miss LePage, there's one thing that bothers me about your interpretation. How can you argue that Whitman's making such a positive statement about the use of drugs when you admit he's suffered from a bad trip, and, furthermore, when the end of the poem is so negative? It seems to me that, if anything, Whitman's going to give up the use of drugs."

"What do you mean?" she asked.

"Well, extending your interpretation a little, wouldn't you say that Whitman's pretty freaked out by the end of the poem?"

"Why?"

"In the last few lines he says, 'I too am not a bit tamed, I too am untranslatable, / I sound my barbaric yawp over the roofs of the world.' Now wouldn't you say he's in pretty bad shape if that's the way he's describing himself—as a 'barbaric yawp'?"

"No, not at all. He's talking about something new here—the new music, acid rock, and a new rock group, 'The Barbaric Yawps.' " And she continued her knitting.

The Secret Life of Huckleberry Finn

"It doesn't seem quite right to me," she said, "to say that Huckleberry Finn is a homosexual."

It was my most loquacious student, Clara LePage, voicing her opinion about a notorious essay on *Huckleberry Finn* by an academician who claimed that Huck and Jim were having a homosexual relationship as they floated down the Mississippi River on their raft. I had mentioned the famous essay and the possibilities of such a relationship, and I was surprised that Miss Le Page hadn't accepted the interpretation, since she rarely missed an erotic undertone or overtone in any work.

"I'm afraid I have to agree with you, Miss LePage," I replied, relieved that for once we would not have to go into a lengthy sexual analysis of the work. And then I added, "It's a rather sexless book."

"Oh, no," she replied. "I don't think that's so at all—it's simply that there isn't anything gay between Huck and Jim."

"You mean someone else then?" I asked her.

"No, not that either. I'm just denying that the book is sexless. There's plenty of sex; it's just that the critics have been so concerned with the homosexual overtones that they've overlooked the possibility of anything else."

"Oh," I replied, adding, "You surely don't mean the Duke and the King, do you?"

"No, forget the homosexual theme completely. Twain was fairly straight, as far as I know, and his book is totally heterosexual."

"Then I fail to see what you're suggesting, Miss LePage. We can, of course, assume that the adults in the novel are having normal sexual relations with each other, but—"

"Can we?" she interrupted.

"Miss LePage," I said, raising my voice a little, "I do wish you'd just say what you mean for once instead of always beating about the bush. I'm certain you're not going to shock anyone in the class."

"What I'm suggesting," Miss LePage replied, "is that there was something going on between Huckleberry Finn and the Widow Douglass, and—"

"The Widow Douglass!" I replied, my voice once again changing several octaves. "Huck Finn's about thirteen or fourteen years old, and she's—she's old enough to be his grandmother—fifty-five, maybe sixty years old. Isn't this all a little farfetched?"

"I don't know why it should be. It's exactly the same

thing in *Lolita*, except that it's an older man and a young girl. If an older man can lust after a young girl, I certainly don't see why an older woman can't be interested in a young man. That's my whole point. You've got to stop placing women in stereotyped roles. You do this with every book we read. The Widow Douglass was quite a passionate woman, and I don't see any reason at all why she can't be regarded as a sex symbol."

"But she may be over sixty years old," I told her, searching the faces of the other students for a kindred soul, for someone who could negate what Miss LePage was saying.

"So is Mae West," she replied.

I thought I was going to see red, and I began to rub my eyes as I felt a throbbing begin in my left temple. "Miss LePage, besides the fact that all of this is absurd, there's absolutely no way you can prove what you're saying from the text. Things like this simply don't happen."

"Pedophilia is a genuine sexual preference, Professor, fully documented. I looked it up in my sex dictionary."

"You mean your dictionary of perversions, don't you?"

She ignored my comment. "Furthermore, there is plenty of proof in the text to support what I'm saying. You simply refuse to see women as anything but passive, neutered objects."

"Would you mind, then, telling us how you came to your interpretation?" I stood there at the lectern in a stupor, my head supported by my hand.

"It's all rather obvious: the way she keeps taking him into the closet to play—I mean to pray. You know as well as I do what's going on there. The reason Huck runs away is simply because he's been seduced by the Widow Douglass, who, since she is a widow, is naturally a little uptight about her situation, shall we say? Why do you suppose she picked him up in the first place?"

"If it's such a good thing, why doesn't Huck stay around and keep it up with her?" I asked, before I realized what I'd said.

"I never said that the relationship was satisfactory from Huck's point of view," Miss LePage replied. "For the Widow Douglass it is, of course. You've forgotten that she even manages to get Huck's Pap to live with her for a time. But for Huckleberry Finn it's something else. After a while, he naturally wants someone a little younger—so he runs away before he becomes a total slave to her passions."

"Miss LePage, do you know anything about Mark Twain himself? Do you think this is the kind of interpretation he would have wanted?"

"Well, Twain, of course, wanted to write a much more blatantly erotic novel, but because of the times and his wife's nagging, he had to conceal some of his intentions. All I'm trying to say is that Huck Finn is a healthy young man—with normal desires. We're not dealing with a David Eisenhower type here, but a boy who simply happens to have a rather frustrating initial sexual experience—with an older woman. So Twain has him run away—in search of a younger girl—and that accounts for all of the later sequences in the novel."

"But you've overlooked so many other things, Miss LePage. Surely you don't expect us to think that all of the other sequences are nothing but Huck's search for a younger girl?"

"You've forgotten that unlike Tom Sawyer, Huck Finn didn't have a Becky Thatcher he could take into the cave anytime he wanted to."

My head felt as if it might explode. "And the racial overtones of the novel—the entire relationship between Huck and Jim—doesn't that have any significance at all, Miss LePage?" I sat there thinking that the homosexual interpretation had suddenly become infinitely preferable to whatever Miss LePage was about to say.

"Of course it does—they're both searching for the same thing—basically, that is. They both ran away, didn't they?"

"I fail to see what you're getting at, Miss LePage. Surely you're not saying that the Widow Douglass was interested in Jim too?"

"No, not exactly. It was her sister, Miss Watson, who was after him. And when he got tired of it all, just like Huck Finn, he too ran away."

"You mean to say that the whole trip on the raft is nothing but an attempt to get away from the two old women? Miss LePage, these interpretations of yours really do get out of hand sometimes."

"What do you mean?"

"They have nothing to do with the work itself. That isn't what an interpretation of a book is supposed to do. You've got to found your theory in some critical school of thought. All you ever do is talk about sex—as if that alone constituted a critical viewpoint. And you're running out of perversions."

"I don't see what's so different from what you're always saying about Freud and Young."

"Jung, not Young! That's exactly what I mean. Let me put it rather bluntly. Have you ever—just once I ask you—heard an English major present the kind of interpretations about these books that you do?"

"But I am an English major," she replied.

"Since when?"

"Since the beginning of the semester when I registered for this course. Didn't you even notice? I checked the box on the form—you're supposed to be my advisor."

Heaven help me, I thought, but I kept my comment to myself. "Well, then, I guess we'd better see that you sign up for the right courses next semester. You're a second-semester junior, aren't you?"

"Yes, but I've checked with the registrar—and I can fit all my required courses in next year. I'll keep my minor in business which will make me interdisciplinary."

"Literature and business?" I asked her.

"Why not? My father publishes books."

God, when would these revelations cease? I felt we had to return to our discussion. "Was there anything else you wanted to say about *Huckleberry Finn?*"

"No, that's all."

"Then I wonder if you'd mind answering just one more question for me, Miss LePage. According to your theory, Jim also runs off because he's being pursued by an older woman. I wonder if you'd mind telling me why, instead of running North, he runs South, where he simply gets deeper and deeper into the heart of slavery? Isn't that a flaw in the novel?"

"I didn't say he was running away from sex itself, Professor, or even from an older woman. It was simply that he'd had it with white women, and in the South he'd have a much better chance of finding a black woman the next time."

Will the Real Emily Dickinson
Please Stand Up?

"How can we be certain that Emily Dickinson really existed?" she asked me, as I paused momentarily during my lecture.

"Who? What do you mean?" I asked her.

"Emily Dickinson. I was just wondering if it wasn't someone else who wrote her poems."

"What do you mean, Miss LePage? Are you suggesting that the poems were the product of some other genius?"

"Yes, I think so. I mean, isn't it possible that someone other than Emily Dickinson wrote them?"

"I suppose it could be possible, but I'd say it's highly improbable, Miss LePage. So unless you think you've come up with something—"

"All I mean, Professor, is that with the scarcity of information about Emily Dickinson—especially her own personal life—isn't there a good chance that she never really existed at all?"

"But she did exist. There's plenty of evidence about that."

"Oh, I know that there was someone with that name," Miss LePage continued, "but don't you think it's a little funny that we know almost nothing about someone who lived as recently as she did? People think that someone else wrote Shakespeare's plays. How can we be certain that the same thing isn't true of Emily Dickinson's poems?"

"You're not suggesting that Shakespeare wrote Emily Dickinson's poems, are you?"

"Of course not—the dates don't work."

"Then what do you mean?"

"Well, there are several possibilities. That's what's so difficult. What I don't understand is why the critics haven't thought about this before. I mean why hasn't this theory been suggested by someone else? There must be something fishy going on. People don't live in a country like ours without leaving a few known facts."

"Yes, yes, yes, I know, Miss LePage, but so far you have failed to illuminate us." I was beginning to feel my usual frustration with the LePagian approach to literature.

"Well, first I thought it might be Edgar Allen Poe, only I threw that out because I think that although it's possible that he didn't die in 1849 as everyone believes, it's highly unlikely that with all that drinking, and the syphilis and everything, he'd last until 1886, when Ms. Dickinson supposedly died. So I don't think that we can assume it was Poe. It was someone else."

"Who—Poe's wife, Virginia Clemm?" I couldn't resist asking.

"I ruled that possibility out, too, though I thought at one stage last night when I was reading the poems that it might be possible. I hadn't finished reading all the poems then."

"You read all of Emily Dickinson's poems last night—all seventeen hundred and seventy-five of them?"

"Well, I did take the speed-reading course last semester," she replied. "I don't know what's so unusual about that. After all, I could hardly make a case for my theory if I hadn't read them at least once, could I? I was just looking for certain images anyway."

"Just what is your thesis, Miss LePage?" I asked her, my tone becoming somewhat sarcastic.

"Well, I've figured it out like this: I'm certain that the poems weren't written by the person who purported to be Emily Dickinson. In fact, there never was a real Emily Dickinson as we think of her, but someone else whom the Dickinsons were sheltering. They were liberals, you know. My first hunch was that the poems were written by a man. As I read through them, however, I realized that they couldn't possibly have been written by a male—unless of course it was someone like Henry James. But I ruled that out, too, because if James had written poems, each one would have been a couple of hundred lines long. So there was only one possibility left."

"Who?"

"Someone who was supposed to have died about the time Emily Dickinson wrote her first poems. Some female who was supposed to be dead, but who was in fact still alive, living under the assumed name of Emily Dickinson, in mourning, wearing white the rest of her life. Do you see what I mean?"

"No, not really. What have you done—found some unknown citizen about whom we know even less?"

"No, of course not. I'm referring to Margaret Fuller."

"Margaret Fuller?"

"Yes, don't you remember? Ms. Fuller supposedly died in 1850, in a shipwreck off Fire Island, when she was forty years old. But it's obvious that she didn't. She assumed the name of Emily Dickinson and continued writing for the rest of her life—only she wrote poems so she could conceal her identity. By 1886, she would have been seventy-six years old. The year of the shipwreck is the year Emily Dickinson wrote her first poems. She's always writing about the sea and drowning. In the early poem with the pretty title "# 52," for example, she says—if I may quote a part of it—' . . . my bark went down at sea.' Don't you understand now? She didn't die; she was simply reborn. It's pure water imagery."

"Miss LePage, there's something here that doesn't make any sense. What would Margaret Fuller have gained from an arrangement like this? I mean, why would she hide her identity for thirty-six years? Don't you think that's a little unlikely?"

"Not at all. I've checked all the facts. Margaret Fuller had a child by an Italian count, but they weren't married. You can imagine how the public would have reacted to her illegitimate child. It's all rather simple; the count and the child died in the shipwreck; Margaret Fuller survived. She didn't have any other choice but to remain in hiding the rest of her life—in mourning."

"But there are so many things you've ignored, Miss LePage. You can't just take a couple of little facts and interpret them like this. You have to use all of the available information, not just a part of it."

"What do you mean? You're just upset because you didn't come up with the theory yourself. In fact, you'll probably publish my idea in a scholarly article some-day."

"Miss LePage, let's be realistic. You haven't proven anything. Your theory is riddled with holes."

"Such as?"

"Well, you just got through saying that Emily Dickinson, I mean Margaret Fuller, lived in mourning all the rest of her life. You know that's not true. She wore white clothes the last thirty years of her life. That's one of the few pieces of information we're certain about. If she were in mourning, she'd be wearing black."

"I'm aware of that," Miss LePage replied. "That's why she wore white. Just like Moby Dick—a reverse symbol. You don't think she wanted everyone to know, do you?"

The Deification of Booker T. Washington

"I expected," Miss LePage began, "that at the end of the book, Washington would ascend into heaven and the earth would ring forth with his canonization."

"Saint Booker T. Washington?" I questioned.

"Why not? Something had to happen to him—he was clearly too good for the earth, though he'd been playing Christ all his life. It almost nauseates me to think about it."

She was referring to *Up from Slavery*, Booker T. Washington's autobiography. Before the class began, Miss LePage had handed me a small brown parcel with the instructions that I shouldn't open it until I got back to my office. And she added, "Why did you ever assign such an awful book?" I didn't have the chance to tell her that it was part of the set reading list for the course.

"The whole thing could never have been written," Miss LePage continued, "if Booker T. hadn't swallowed most of the Bible and Horatio Alger. Why, Booker T. is little more than the story of Christ with a happy ending. Strive and succeed—that's what I mean. I kept expecting Washington to give an account of his birth—Immaculate Conception or something—and that the book would end as he entered into heaven. The imagery of the last chapter is simply too much: 'Last Words' he calls it. I'd call it the Last Supper—without any soul food."

"Miss LePage, your interpretation doesn't make much sense. I mean, after all, the book is an autobiography, and you're talking about it as if it were a novel—as if Washington never actually existed."

"Did he?" she questioned, but immediately continued, "I admit that I wondered that any number of times as I read the book. I was beginning to think that this was the first autobiography ever written by someone who didn't exist."

"Don't you think you're being a little hard on Washington?" I asked her. "The next thing you'll say is that he was secretly married to Emily Dickinson."

She ignored my remark. "We're not exactly dealing with the *Autobiography of Booker X*. In fact," she continued, "I have a perverse feeling that the whole thing was written as some kind of joke."

"In what way, Miss LePage?"

"I almost hesitate to say." There was a pause, and then she said, "Black humor."

"You mean *black*/black humor, don't you?" I asked her.

"Well, if you want to be technical about it. In any case, it's all rather dirty when you start trying to analyze the images."

"I had hoped that this was one book you would find free from that subject."

"Oh, this isn't exactly what you think. I mean with a mind like that constantly regressing to the oral/anal stages, it does get to be a bit heavy. I'd hesitate to say what Freud would have written about Washington, if he'd read the book."

"Miss LePage," I said, "there must be more to life than Freud."

"All I'm saying, Professor, is that with the kind of toothbrush fixation Booker T. Washington had, there must have been something wrong with him. His 'Gospel of the Toothbrush,' as he refers to it, gets to be a little disgusting the tenth or twentieth time around. Can you imagine an autobiography where the central image is the toothbrush? It's almost as if he were using it as a substitute for something else; sometimes I even wonder if he took it to bed with him. Washington's concern with oral hygiene makes him sound a little bit like the world's first toothpaste commercial; but then, as if that isn't enough, he has to proceed to the other orifices too. It would have been better if he'd called his book *Orifice in the Underworld*. How can you explain someone's writing in an autobiography, 'I never see a filthy yard that I do not want to clean'? Surely that's not to be taken literally? No wonder black people are uptight about him."

"Well, this is all pretty strange, Miss LePage, but I wouldn't say it sheds any original light on Washington himself. Is there anything anyone else would care to add?" I asked, looking at the rest of the class.

But it was Miss LePage who answered my question. "Was Washington a Communist?"

"A Communist?" I asked her. "Whatever gave you that idea?"

"The whole picture of Tuskegee," she replied. "It's right out of Marx or Engels. I thought for a while that the book had been ghost-written by Karl Marx or someone—until I checked and saw that Marx was dead by that time. It's propaganda. Collectivism, pure and simple. Five-year plans—although they aren't referred to exactly as that. Everyone doing his thing: making bricks together in the morning, farming, constructing privies. Washington ran Tuskegee as a commune. I'm surprised the whites in the community stood for it. It's a good thing Ronald Reagan wasn't around in those days."

"Miss LePage, all you're doing is taking a few isolated facts from the book and distorting them so that they'll fit your interpretation. Is that really fair? Should literary criticism do that?"

"I thought that's what literary criticism always did," she replied, a little too coy for my own appreciation—"at least the New Critics. I've been careful to stay within the book; but a toothbrush is a toothbrush in spite of what you do with it; a privy is a privy; and no matter what you say, Tuskegee was plain and simple Communism."

"You're hardly a New Critic, Miss LePage," I replied. "If anything, I'd say that you belong to the slap-bang school of literary criticism. And you haven't actually told us anything particularly revealing about Booker T. Washington," I said, my voice slightly tired of it all. "So he brushed his teeth after each meal; so he had everyone at the school working at some kind of manual labor—it was a matter of simple economics. He had to do it that way or he would never have built the school as he did. You have to look at the book in its historical context—and the financial difficulties he had to overcome. A Marxist interpretation might be applicable here, if you would work it out in a little more detail."

"Christian Marxism, then," she replied, "though I don't think Booker T. resembled Christ as much as he did Moses—a kind of black child in the promised land. You don't suppose Booker T. was Jewish, do you?"

J. Alfred Prufrock
and the Prostitute

"Prufrock's not a prude at all," she said. "That's an unfair interpretation. His experiences with women have been many and varied. He's simply out looking for a prostitute."

"What?" I said, surprised at her statement. Had she actually made her point all at once?

Inwardly I knew, however, that we were going to have another one of those classes—until Miss LePage finished unveiling another one of her neurotic interpretations, ruining forever my appreciation of a piece of literature. The month before, she had handed me a brown parcel and told me not to open it until I got to my office. Which I did—hardly able to contain my anxiety. The contents? A pair of brown-and-red socks, hand-knitted, and a card that said "Happy Birthday."

I was doubly confused. How had she known it was my birthday? Why a pair of socks? I'd been trying to figure out her motives ever since then—especially the pair of socks. *Did Oedipus sleep with his socks on?* Was I the object of an infatuation? A seduction? I didn't know what to say ("Thanks for the socks"?), so I'd been trying to avoid her ever since, hoping she would either be absent from class or at least not try to dominate the discussion.

No such luck. She was at it again. I could imagine T.S. Eliot waking up in his tomb, wishing that he'd never written "The Love Song of J. Alfred Prufrock."

"Prufrock, you say, is looking for a prostitute?" I asked her, noting that no one in the class seemed the least bit flabbergasted. It was as if this was the interpretation they had all been waiting for.

"Yes. Look at the opening lines of the poem. It's the most obvious there—the walk through the deserted streets, the references to restless nights in cheap hotels, even the patient etherized on the table. The entire poem is nothing but Prufrock's wanderings around Soho trying to find a prostitute who'll spend the night with him."

"Well, that really shouldn't be so difficult, should it?" I asked her.

"Not normally, but there is one minor complication. He's got to find a prostitute he's never been with before."

"Why—why is that, Miss LePage?" I asked her, wondering if we were talking about the same poem.

"It's a rather delicate matter, Professor. I don't know if I can articulate exactly what I want to say. You see, Prufrock is getting along in years, and that, of course, is some of it, and he's always had this reputation among the prostitutes of London as being a kind of sexual athlete, let's say. I don't mean that he's perverted or anything, but—"

"Prufrock—a sexual athlete?" I interrupted, again unable to control my surprise.

"If you look at the poem very carefully," Miss LePage continued, "you'll see that it's all there. As Eliot says of Prufrock in one place, 'I have known them all already, known them all.' It may sound a little as if he's from Brooklyn, but the point is that Prufrock has acquired a certain renown among the prostitutes of the area. The references to bare arms, and to the light brown hair in the lamplight—aren't they all fairly obvious?"

"No, not exactly. I mean you're not actually supporting your theory. You say he's got to find a prostitute he's never been with before, but you haven't really explained why."

There was a pause, and then she said, "He's got VD."

If I had been upset before, I was now utterly dumfounded and thoroughly chagrined in front of everyone in the class. She had simply used that trick too many times before. "Do all the rest of you think he's got VD, too?" I questioned. "Or just Miss LePage?"

No answer. Not even a giggle. Heads buried in their books so I wouldn't call on them.

"Miss LePage," I continued, raising my voice to a much higher pitch, "how do you explain just about everything else in the poem? The references to the women and Michelangelo, for instance?"

"That's easy. Those are the women Prufrock would *like* to be with. You see, there are some complications.

It's the women who talk of Michelangelo and the women who have tea parties whom Prufrock hasn't had any experiences with. Unfortunately, Prufrock's got some kind of hangup, and he can only enjoy sex with a prostitute."

"But you say he's got a disease. If that's so, don't you imagine he got it from one of those women?"

"Of course, but he's still worried about it, so he'd just as soon find someone who doesn't recognize him. That's what accounts for all the hesitation on his part— the continual references to time and indecisions. Remember that this is 1914 and we're hardly out of Victorian England. Plus the fact, as I said, that he's getting older and more concerned about his physical appearance. A little vain, you might say."

"Do you mean that's why he feels the women will say, 'But how his arms and legs are thin'?" I asked her, proud that I could quote from the poem without looking at the text.

"I think we can safely assume that Prufrock's talking about something besides his legs and arms there," she answered, then added quickly, "speaking metaphorically, of course. It's just like at the beginning, where Eliot describes the fog in such detail. The fog isn't fog at all, of course, but a word substitution on Eliot's part. And if you substitute 'prostitute' for 'fog' as you read the poem, you can see that the meaning is something quite in keeping with what I'm saying."

"If you substitute any other word for 'fog' you get a different meaning also, Miss LePage: aardvark, pomegranate, yellow fever. All you're doing is substituting words—and ruining the poem in the process."

"It's a highly loaded piece of poetry, Professor."

"I have never doubted that, Miss LePage, but I

simply cannot go along with this interpretation. Prufrock's an old man—afraid of women and his own shadow. A little odd, perhaps, but completely inexperienced with women. As you know he even says, "I grow old . . . I grow old . . ./ I shall wear the bottoms of my trousers rolled.' Why, according to your interpretation, he's trying to show off his legs or his socks . . ."

I had the uncanny feeling that Miss LePage was looking at my feet to see if I was wearing the socks she had knit for me. (I wasn't.) Then she came to my rescue. If the other students hadn't been in the classroom, I believe I would have bent over and rolled up my trousers.

"Well," she said, "maybe I'm all wrong about him. You know how difficult it is to get to understand some people—no matter how hard you try."

I swallowed a couple of gulps of air, wondering when I could restore some kind of order to my mind. Then I said, "Should we return to the poem, Miss LePage? Suppose you tell us whom Prufrock's talking to throughout the entire poem, when he says, 'Let us go then, you and I.' Whom is he addressing?"

"I was worried about that myself," she replied. "First I thought it was a pimp, and then I thought it was a madam in a whorehouse, but after reading the poem a second time, I realized it was someone else."

"Who?" I asked her, getting prepared for whatever she would say.

"Ezra Pound."

"Ezra Pound? Why Ezra Pound?"

"Well, Prufrock, of course, is Eliot's alter ego; and Eliot knew that the only way he could keep Pound from editing the poem was by putting him in it. Ingenious, don't you think?"

A Farewell to Hemingway's What?

"**W**as Hemingway trying to imitate Henry James when he wrote *A Farewell to Arms?*" she asked me.

"Imitate Henry James?" I replied. "Why, the two writers couldn't be farther apart."

It was the last week of the semester. The week before, when she came in to get her fall schedule approved, I convinced Miss LePage that she needed to enroll in a Literary Criticism course, so she would have some idea of what literary criticism is supposed to do. That and Major British Writers, which she should have taken as a sophomore. Her other courses would be up to her.

AMERICAN LITERATURE (FALL/SPRING)

"I'm not going to take your course in the Puritans," she had mumbled, turning up her nose at me a little, as if the idea itself smelled. "So I guess that means that I won't be taking a course from you next fall." In a way, I was relieved—I would finally be free of her.

"Have you something against the Puritans, Miss LePage?" I asked her.

"Why do you have to teach the dullest course in the department? How could you ever make that your specialty?"

"The graduate students don't find it that dull, Miss LePage. Perhaps you're just a little young to appreciate the subject."

"You couldn't get me to take that course for all the tea in China," she replied. So we left it at that. In the fall, she would be nineteen, a senior in English—taking five courses in the department, driving five of my colleagues crazy. At least from now on she'd be someone else's problem.

I stood there in front of the class, smiling a little, relishing the thought that this was the last nonsensical dialogue we would have. *A Farewell to Arms* and a farewell to Miss LePage.

"After everything I've always heard about Hemingway," she said, "I thought he'd at least be a little more with it."

"What do you mean, Miss LePage?" I asked, curious, I admit, to see what her interpretation would be.

"Well, I assumed there would be a little more sex in the novel. Hemingway's a twentieth-century writer, but he's no more liberated than Hawthorne and Melville. *A Farewell to Arms* isn't nearly as exciting as the book you assigned for my outside paper: Nathanael West's *Miss*

Lonelyparts."

"Please, Miss LePage, spare me!"

"Hemingway's more of a Puritan than all the other writers we've read. That's what bothers me so much. *A Farewell to Arms* could have been written by Henry James—all you'd have to do is run a few sentences together."

"I'd say your comment is a little farfetched, Miss LePage. Have you forgotten some of the other books we've read already? Here at least the whole conflict, you might say, grows out of a love affair. After all, Catherine Barkley dies in childbirth. She is pregnant."

"I'm not so certain about that. Maybe she just blows up," Miss LePage replied. "Don't you see what I mean? People are always saying that Hemingway's anti-women, but that's not the half of it. He's anti-sex—*against sex*. Why, you might call *A Farewell to Arms* propaganda for birth control: no sex at all is even better than the rhythm method. The end of the novel fully supports this. Catherine Barkley dies because she's led a loose life; she isn't married. Why, it's the most didactic ending I've ever read. Nathaniel Hawthorne would never have had Hester die off like that. Even Henry James was never that much of a moralist. I just don't see what people find to admire in an attitude toward sex as puritanical as Hemingway's."

"Aren't you negating the pregnancy a little, Miss LePage?" I asked her, hoping that I could force her to examine the substance of the novel a little more closely.

"I think we can say that Catherine's pregnancy is the most misunderstood aspect of the novel."

"In what way?"

"The child isn't Frederick Henry's at all, but someone else's. He's never even slept with her—that's what makes him such a boob. I've never seen such a guilt-ridden character as Frederick Henry. And Catherine's death is the cheapest trick of all—*deus ex machismo*, I guess I'd call it. Hemingway kills her off so he can save Frederick Henry's face."

"Miss LePage, surely you don't expect us to believe your interpretation, do you?"

"Well, it's all there in the book, Professor, if you just study the text rather carefully."

"About the child, Miss LePage?" I asked her, wondering if we were talking about the same novel.

"About the fact that it isn't Henry's. She's really taken him for a ride, you know."

"I'm afraid I didn't know that, Miss LePage. Could you explain what you mean?"

"Well, if you'll look at page 79, you'll see that James—I mean Hemingway—says, 'Catherine Barkley was generally liked by the nurses because she would do night duty indefinitely.' That's what it's all about, Professor. Nurse Barkley's been sleeping around with everyone but Henry. It's some other soldier who's got her into her fix. Later on she even says to him—if I may quote from the novel again—'I wish we could do something really sinful.' But it doesn't work. Every time she starts to make a pass at him, he turns around and starts feeling guilty about his sexual desires. That's what makes me conclude that Hemingway's males are a bunch of big babies. This whole Hemingway masculinity cult only works when there are no females around. In one of the Nick Adams stories, Nick breaks up with his girl friend because she's learned to fish as well as he can. Have you ever heard of anything more infantile? If that's masculinity, you can have it. I mean, can you actually imagine a Hemingway character getting married and living happily ever after?"

"Miss LePage, this is the most absurd interpretation I've ever heard of this book. Did you finish reading the novel?"

"Look at Hemingway's own life—his four marriages. Every time one of his wives had a child, he divorced her. Hemingway hated that name Papa, and he was damn certain no little brat was going to call Frederick Henry 'Papa.' What I mean is that it's bad enough to call the book anti-sex. But it's even worse when you realize it's pro-celibacy. Why, I read better nurse novels when I was in junior high school, and you know that's what we're really dealing with here—nothing more than another nurse novel. He should have called it *Nurse Barkley's American Episode.*"

"Aren't you forgetting that the real significance of the novel is Hemingway's radical anti-war statement, Miss LePage? You haven't even mentioned the war at all. As usual, all you've done is quote a few passages from the text and distort the meaning of the work."

"The war is mere backdrop, Professor. Coincidence, you might say. There's a war going on in almost every nurse novel."

"Then what about the title, Miss LePage? Why did Hemingway call it *A Farewell to Arms?* What about the ending and the rain symbolism?" I asked, thinking that I had finally stumped her.

"Well, if Catherine is dead at the end of the story, he certainly isn't going to have to worry about her grabbing him anymore, is he?"

"And the rain?"

AMERICAN LITERATURE (FALL/SPRING)

"Hemingway stole that from Shakespeare. Frederick Henry's still trying to wash himself of the whole affair. Frankly, I felt like taking a bath when I got to the end of the novel."

PART THREE

Major British Writers
(fall/spring)

Beowulf's Hangup

"**W**as Beowulf married?" a voice from the back of the room asked me.

"What?" I replied, already noticing the tremble in my voice.

"Was Beowulf married?" she repeated.

I knew at once that it was Miss LePage, but I didn't know how she had discovered that I was teaching a section of Major British Writers, since my name hadn't been listed in the catalogue. I had, in fact, agreed to teach the course early in September—just before the semester began—after one of my colleagues had a nervous breakdown.

111

It was the second meeting of the semester, and the students were supposed to have read *Beowulf.* I was certain that Miss LePage had not been there for the first class—I had in fact signed her registration card at the end of the spring semester and placed her in another section. So at first I thought I was imagining the whole thing. Then I looked at her more closely (red hair, grown longer over the summer, more mature) and realized there was little doubt—I was stuck with her for another year (albeit a final one). She was a senior now, nineteen years old, an English major; barring any catastrophe, she would graduate in the spring. I started to light a cigarette; already I was wondering what she would do the following week with *Sir Gawain and the Green Knight.*

"Was he?" It was the third time she had asked her question. I couldn't remember that she'd ever been that persistent.

"I don't think so," I replied, nearly burning my fingers with the match. "It's difficult to tell. No, I guess not. The textual evidence—"

"That's what I thought," she replied, as I managed to get my cigarette lit.

"Does it matter?" I asked her, trying to pass off her question as a trivial point, hoping she had nothing else to add, yet knowing that whatever she'd dreamed up would probably ruin discussion for the rest of the period.

"Haven't you ever thought about it before?" she demanded, looking at the students around her, yet clearly aiming her question at me. She had, of course, managed to get the attention of the rest of the students, whose names I had not yet learned. The mood of the class was clearly such that no one was going to say a word before he heard what else Miss LePage had to say.

"Okay," I answered her, thinking the frontal approach would be the least difficult. "What's the reason Beowulf never married?"

"Well," she started, in what I assumed was her most serious tone, "I don't know if this is the only reason, but it's fairly obvious after reading the work that he's a homosexual."

No noise. No giggles. Nothing. They were immune. The other students sat there in their blobbish collectiveness. They might just as well have been made of plastic. Nothing turned them on. Maybe I should be happy to have an occasional student as alive as Miss LePage. There was nothing to do but ask the logical question.

"How can you tell? How do you know?" I said, conscious that my voice showed that I was not keeping my cool.

"Well, if from nothing else, by just about everything he does. I mean, haven't you ever paid attention to the little things Beowulf's always doing throughout the whole story?"

"Perhaps I haven't, Miss LePage," I confessed, exhaling smoke from my mouth. "Such as?"

"Oh, you know, like always putting his arms around everyone—I mean all the other males in the story."

"You're being absurd," I told her, feeling the blood rush to my face.

"I'm serious. You're just not very observant," she continued, almost as if I hadn't said anything. "Didn't you ever notice that when Beowulf kills someone, he does it by hugging him to death? That he's always got to have his arms around some other male?"

One of the other students was nodding his head—a little as if someone were controlling it by a string from up above. I thought he was going to say something, but he didn't. My eyes went back to Miss LePage.

"Can you imagine anything so stupid as getting undressed when he knows he's going to have to fight Grendel? I mean, after all, Heorot Hall isn't exactly the safest place to spend a night—and yet the first thing Beowulf does when he gets there is take his clothes off. The text says, if I may read it for you,

> *He stripped off his shirt, his helmet, his sword*
> *Hammered from the hardest iron, and handed*
> *All his weapons and armor to a servant.*

Don't you think that's fairly clear?"

"But he knew his strength," I told her. "He was going to crush Grendel to death." I put my cigarette out in an empty coffee cup.

"Then why doesn't he do the same thing with Grendel's mother?" she asked. "When he goes off to kill her, he's decked out in all the armor he can find. He doesn't fight her all stripped down like that—he's afraid to touch a woman."

I lit another cigarette. There didn't seem to be much else I could do. Her imagination was endless.

"He's simply got a thing for males. He's always swimming naked with other young men—like Brecca, for instance. And he has a passion for hugging them. If you remember, that's the way he kills the dragon too."

"Was it a male dragon?" I asked her. Someone in the room snickered, but I couldn't tell who it was. My eyes felt a little as if they had lost their sensitivity to light. I released a sigh of cigarette smoke, wondering how I'd ever get the discussion back to normality.

"So what's your point?" I finally asked her.

"Well, I think it's pretty clear. Beowulf was gay— and if you look at the poem that way the whole meaning's

114

changed. He's not the one you're supposed to sympathize with."

"Who then—Grendel?" I asked, continuing the dialogue to its illogical end.

"Grendel's mother. Who else? She's the one we're supposed to feel sorry for. Grendel was an only child. His poor mother. What really bothers Beowulf—and the reason he puts all that stuff on before he goes to fight her—is that a female has come to avenge Grendel's death. It's too humiliating. If it had been Grendel's father instead—"

"Grendel doesn't have a father," I told her, almost at the end of my patience.

"How do you know?"

"There's no textual evidence," I replied, knowing I was pulling punches with her.

"There isn't any textual evidence that he doesn't, either," she replied.

"Anything else you've got on your mind now that you've ruined the poem for us?" I asked her.

"Just one thing."

"What?"

"I think Beowulf's lack of masculinity is beyond question at the end of the tale."

"How?"

"Well, usually when a hero in an epic does some sort of great heroic deed, he's given a boon, isn't he?"

"He *is*," I answered her, "all that treasure—or did you ignore it?"

"That's exactly my point. It should have been a woman. Why didn't Hrothgar give Beowulf a young maiden for killing Grendel, if he was such a brave young man? Hrothgar knew he was gay."

"So he lives happily ever after—childless," I replied with a little too obvious a sneer.

"Hrothgar knows what's going on. That's why he sends him away. You think he wants someone around his court who's a fetishist?"

"A fetishist?" I asked her, wondering what she was talking about. "Whatever are you referring to?"

"The arm," she replied. "Grendel's arm—didn't you see how Beowulf tried to keep it?"

Key to *The Canterbury Tales*

"Has anyone ever suggested that the Canterbury pilgrims aren't on a religious pilgrimage at all, but are going somewhere else?" she asked me.

"Only you, Miss LePage," I replied. "You're the only one I've heard make that suggestion, though I once heard a student say that the Wife of Bath was from Liverpool."

It was Clara LePage speaking again. In the three weeks since the semester had begun, I had learned that when she discovered I was teaching Major British Writers, she had dropped out of the section she was enrolled in and added mine.

"So where do you think they're going, if they aren't on their way to Canterbury?" I asked her.

"Well, I can't be certain of their true destination, but I do feel that it's clear that there aren't supposed to be any religious overtones to *The Canterbury Tales.*"

"Haven't you forgotten that a number of the pilgrims are members of the church, Miss LePage? The nun, for instance?"

"Oh, well, that's easily explained by the times. Traveling wasn't exactly easy in Chaucer's time. Several of the women put on disguises of one sort or another. Single women were likely to be raped by highwaymen. I think that's why so many of them traveled incognito."

"Who, for instance, Miss LePage?" I asked her, looking around the class to see if any of the students were interested in what was being said. But they weren't.

"The most obvious example is the Wife of Bath—I mean the woman *disguised* as the Wife of Bath."

"You mean she's not a wife from Bath?" I asked her, my mouth temporarily coming unhinged. I lit a cigarette to calm my nerves.

"No—she's the only real nun in the group. You see, she's an old nun who knows quite well that if she travels wearing a habit, she'll be raped. Highwaymen always raped nuns, because they thought they had the chance to get a virgin that way. So she disguised herself as a foul-mouthed woman of the world, while in truth she's the only virgin in the entire group. She knows that if she pretends that she's had five husbands, no one will make a pass at her. You can tell that it's all a put-on when she says, 'No one can be so bold—I mean no man—/ At lies and swearing as a woman can.' "

"This is a rather dubious analysis, if I may say so, Miss LePage. But assuming this is so, then how do you account for the women who actually are traveling as nuns? Wouldn't that disprove your interpretation?"

"Not at all—they're the ones who *want* to be seduced. So they've purposely dressed up that way."

"—"

I didn't know what to say. She'd figured it all out, and I had to admit that some of what she'd said made sense. I cleared my throat, looking around to see what effect her remark was having on the other students. They probably hadn't read the tales. "Well, then, Miss LePage, getting back to your theory that they aren't going on a religious pilgrimage, I suppose you've got a reason for that too?"

"It's just as obvious. Who ever heard of such a group of crooks and lecherous old men going on a religious pilgrimage? All you have to do is think about it for a few minutes and you realize that these aren't the kind of people likely to be doing that."

"So where are they going, Miss LePage? To an encounter group meeting?"

"No, don't be ridiculous. The internal evidence seems to suggest something about horses. My guess is that they're going to a horse race—so they can bet on the horses. I mean, it's just that they're all so familiar with horses that—"

"Well, they are riding horses, Miss LePage. They're certainly not walking to Canterbury—or wherever they're going." I added that last remark before I had the chance to catch myself. "But where is all this leading us, anyway, Miss LePage? So they aren't going to Canterbury or on a religious pilgrimage. The tales still exist in the format we have them in, you know. You can't deny that, can you?"

"I wasn't trying to do that, Professor. In fact, that's

119

what I wanted to get at—the organization of the tales themselves—the format, as you've referred to it."

"Oh?" I asked her, more curious than I should have permitted myself to be.

"Yes, I think maybe I've discovered the key to the organization of *The Canterbury Tales.* I think that they serve as the archetypal patterns for almost all of our later English literature."

"That's nothing that hasn't been suggested before, Miss LePage. After all, they do come before just about everything else—except for *Beowulf,* of course."

"I mean archetypally in a rather primitive way, Professor, as folk tales of a heathen people, recorded by Chaucer, who acts as a precursor of later recorders of folk literature—someone like Lévi-Strauss, for example. If you make a generative transformational analysis of the individual tales, it's possible to—"

"A what, Miss LePage?" I interrupted her. Already I was beginning to wish I hadn't insisted that she take that course in literary criticism. (In a paper she had written the week before, she had defended the linguistic approach used by Lévi-Strauss, Gnome Chomsky, and others.)

"A generative transformational analysis of the problems and solutions posed in each of the tales, a structural approach to determine the individual components of each tale in the sequence—then it's possible to illustrate how all subsequent English literature flows out of these tales. Do you see what I mean?"

"I'm afraid I don't have the slightest idea what you're talking about, Miss LePage. Isn't this getting rather far removed from the literary significance of the tales themselves?"

"Not at all. Let me show you what I mean. All you do is analyze each tale according to the conflict and the solution. For example, to use the terminology used by structuralists, the problem or conflict is thought of as something lacking and therefore carries the symbol L for 'lack.' The solution, or attempt toward a solution, is either called a 'move' or in some cases a 'countermove,' indicated by the symbols M and C. So if you take a tale like 'The Miller's Tale'—one of the dirty ones that you forgot to assign us, by the way—the analysis would be $L + M + A = S$. The A is a symbol for 'artifice' or trickery, and the S stands for the solution. Don't you see how easy it is? All you do is assign the proper symbols for each move and countermove in the tale—and all its other component parts." She stopped talking and sat there smiling—clearly satisfied with her analysis of "The Miller's Tale."

"But this doesn't make any sense, Miss LePage. So you can come up with a formula for each tale. What good does it do us?" I put my cigarette out in an ash tray and lit another one.

"You get a simplified formula for each complex literary work, reducing a work of literature to its basic linguistic components. Once this is done, a reader doesn't have to bother about the tale any longer; all he has to do is look at the symbols. They eliminate the superficial literary descriptions which might sidetrack a reader from objective research. For example, what's the point of a descriptive passage in a work such as 'The Miller's Tale'? The formula, you see, simply leaves it out and gets to the heart of the matter. It enables us to analyze literature much more easily, much faster—without having to bother to read the work itself. Slow readers can read a work much faster this way—once they're familiar with the symbols."

"Miss LePage, do you know what I think? I think that all of this is insane, but if you feel that it's important to our discussion, perhaps you'd be so good as to analyze one of the tales I did assign, so all the rest of us will know its formula, just in case we don't want to read the entire work the next time around. Could you do this for us by using 'The Wife of Bath's Tale,' for example?"

"That's the easiest one of all. There's no real lack in this tale, so we omit the L symbol. We start, instead, with the first move—when the squire from King Arthur's Court rapes the girl. If I may digress a minute, you'll notice that the Wife of Bath, that is, the old nun, subconsciously has no control over her thoughts. A nun dresses as an old hag from Bath, because she's afraid she'll be raped if her true identity is known; nevertheless, she tells a tale in which rape is central. But to get back to the formula, the squire's move is the initial rape. He's afraid he'll be punished for what he's done, but the queen gives him a chance to save himself—all he has to do is find out what women most desire in life and tell her. She thinks he won't be able to do this. But he outfoxes her in his countermove, by asking the person least likely to know the answer to the queen's question—an old hag. She tells him that what women most desire in life is control over their husbands. Since that's a countermove which cancels out the original move in this case, we put a 2 above it, or a C^2."

"But what about everything else in the tale, Miss LePage? You said earlier that additional symbols are necessary to complete the formula of each tale. In 'The Wife of Bath's Tale,' for example, we have a rather lascivious intent on the part of the woman who tells the tale—possibly to arouse some of her listeners, if I may develop what you've already said about her."

"Well, then you assign an E to that, Professor," she said.

"An E? What for?"

"The symbol for dirty stories is E, for erotic, since that seems to be the prime intent for including this story in *The Canterbury Tales*. Don't you see?"

I sat there with a rather perplexed look on my face. "Surely you don't mean what you've just said, do you, Miss LePage?"

"In what way?" she asked me.

"This is preposterous, Miss LePage. The M for move and the C^2 for the countermove results in the E for erotic? The formula you've just given for 'The Wife of Bath's Tale' is $E = MC^2$."

"Well, I never said that the linguistic method was foolproof, Professor."

How Shakespeare Wrote His Sonnets

"Do you happen to know what the penalty was for plagiarism in Shakespeare's day?" she asked.

"It's a well-known fact, Miss LePage," I told her, "that Shakespeare borrowed from a number of sources for his plays—Plutarch's *Lives* and Holinshed's *Chronicles*, for example. Material that was in the public domain. So I don't think you could really call it plagiarism."

"I was referring to the sonnets," she replied. "Everybody knows where he got the material for his plays. I was wondering if he might not have plagiarized someone else's work, since the inconsistencies seem to indicate a very hackneyed job."

"Will you explain yourself, Miss LePage? I'm certain we'd all like to know who *really* wrote Shakespeare's works." I glanced around, hoping to notice some reaction on the students' faces—but it appeared that they didn't care at all about the mysterious element of authenticity in the Bard's work. All, that is, except for one student who I thought had cringed at the word "plagiarism." I looked at him for another moment and noticed that he was beginning to turn a deep red.

"Well, it's not authorship that I really meant. I mean, I don't think they were written by Sir Walter Raleigh or Queen Elizabeth or an IBM machine or any of that kind of nonsense. To find that out, we'll just have to wait until we get to the Great Library Reference Room in the Sky—"

"The what?" I interrupted her.

"The Great Library Reference Room in the Sky— the afterlife. It's nothing more than a big library, but with books that tell the truth. You check out the yearbook for 1963 and it will tell you who really killed Kennedy. We'll be able to learn who wrote Shakespeare's plays. Whether Homer was a man or a woman. Or look at a picture of the Loch Ness monster."

"Oh." I stood there rather flabbergasted. I lit a cigarette in anticipation of her upcoming remarks.

"What I meant was that I thought the sonnets might be the result of *intentional* plagiarism. Shakespeare never really wanted to write sonnets in the first place— they were simply in vogue. Everybody was doing it, so he had to write some too. Only he took the easiest way out—and plagiarized all of them, stealing a line here and

125

a line there, and constructing new sonnets in the process.
But—"

"Now wait a minute, Miss LePage," I interrupted
her. "You're going a little too far. You can't say things
like that without giving some evidence to support
your—your theories, I guess you'd call them. What do
you mean Shakespeare stole a line here and a line there
and then constructed 'new sonnets'?"

"I figured it all out, Professor, when I read them
over last night. All the tomfoolery that's been written
about the sonnets is nothing more than the inability of the
critics to understand the absurd nature of the poet's
practice of plagiarism in the first place. Plagiarism is the
one explanation for all of the inconsistencies in Shakespeare's sonnet sequence—his supposed bisexuality expressed in love for the mysterious Dark Lady and the
unnamed young man."

"You're going way too fast for me, Miss LePage.
I've lost your train of thought."

"It's very simple. The irregularities in Shakespeare's sonnets are the sole result of faulty—or should I
say hurried—plagiarism. After all, Shakespeare did
know how to plagiarize effectively when he wanted to,
even if he couldn't rely on *Cliff's Notes*. During those lost
years when he was teaching, he'd seen enough examples
of student plagiarism to prepare him for a great literary
career. The plays were always ideas he'd stolen from
someone else, and we accept them because they're great
literature, beautiful language. But the sonnets are
another thing."

"You still haven't given any proof that a word of
what you've said is true, Miss LePage." I waited for
some reaction from the other students, but there was

none, except for the red-faced boy, whose skin had changed to a deep purple. Before the class had begun he had handed me a late paper, and now he kept glancing at it on the end of the table where I'd placed it. "Can you give us just a mite of evidence?" I asked her, anxious to return to my earlier discussion.

"Well, my theory—if you want to call it that—is that Shakespeare simply 'translated' parts of other sonnets from the Italian sonneteers and reworked them into sonnets that he passed off as his own. Mostly from Petrarch and other Italian poets, but a few English writers, too, such as Thomas Wyatt and Sir Philip Sidney. Shakespeare took a line or two from one sonnet and added it to a line or two from another until he'd got the required fourteen lines, and then he called it his own. It's all so simple that anyone could do it in a few hours. I'm surprised no one ever figured it out."

"If it's so simple to do, then why hasn't anyone else ever done it, Miss LePage?" I asked her.

"Well, I can't be accountable for that. I suppose no one else wanted to—after all, sonnets aren't exactly 'in' these days—perhaps that's why they went out so quickly after Shakespeare's time. I dare say anyone could construct a sonnet that way."

"In that case, Miss LePage, perhaps you'd be so good as to write one that way for our next class," I said, determined to silence her. "And now if that's the end of your theory, perhaps we could return to our discussion."

"I have one here that I constructed last night," Miss LePage replied, before I could say anything else to get our discussion going again. "Would you like me to read it now?"

What could I say? I'd fallen into her trap once again.

I couldn't detect a note of interest on the faces of the other students—except for the one who had turned purple a few minutes earlier. I thought he was slowly sliding under the table. I wondered if I should ask if he was ill.

"Well, then," she began, "I've constructed this sonnet—which I call 'Shakespeare's Sonnet Number 155,' giving full credit where it's due—by stealing fourteen lines from Shakespeare's sequence of a hundred and fifty-four sonnets. You'll notice that I have retained the proper rhyme scheme and that this sonnet makes about as much sense as any of the others in the series—perhaps more." And she read:

> *Oaths of thy love, thy truth, thy constancy*
> *Which have no correspondence with true sight:*
> *For all that beauty that doth cover thee,*
> *O'ercharged with burthen of mine own love's might.*
> *In our two loves there is but one respect,*
> *Where beauty's veil doth cover every blot;*
> *The ornament of beauty is suspect,*
> *Thou mayst be false, and yet I know it not.*
> *So shall I live, supposing thou art true,*
> *Not that the summer is less pleasant now:*
> *No marvel, then, though I mistake my view,*
> *With all-triumphant splendour on my brow:*
> *Look, what is best, that best I wish in thee,*
> *Make thee another self, for love of me.* *

"Do you want me to explicate it, Professor?" she asked, after she had finished reading it aloud.

"No, I don't think that will be necessary, Miss Le

*Readers concerned about Miss LePage's scholarship will find the sources of these lines in the following of Shakespeare's sonnets: 152, 148, 22, 23, 36, 95, 70, 92, 93, 102, 148, 33, 37, and 10.

Page," I replied, wondering what I should say next. The purple student had vanished under the table while she was reading her poem. I thought I could hear him rummaging around among the other students' feet.

"It's all so very easy to write sonnets this way, Professor—if you just have the patience. I think I've found the answer to all the unanswered questions surrounding Shakespeare's sonnets. The reason why he couldn't finish Number 126, for example—the one that only has twelve lines in it—was because he couldn't find two more lines to finish it with. And—"

"Miss LePage?" I questioned, hoping to interrupt her monologue.

"—the young man in the sonnets and the Dark Lady can easily be explained because Shakespeare stole some lines from homosexual sonnets and some from heterosexual ones. Of course, the real explanation for the Dark Lady is that she's Petrarch's Laura—since so many of the lines were taken from his sonnets. She'd have to be dark, since she's from southern Italy. And the 'W.H.' in the dedication that has puzzled scholars for years can be explained by—"

"Miss LePage, couldn't—" I repeated futilely as a purple hand shot up over the edge of the table and removed the paper from in front of me. "Miss LePage!"

But she rambled on, "—Shakespeare wasn't really interested in sex much anyway—in spite of the Dark Lady and the young man. That's why he fudged on his sonnets. He was straight as an arrow."

What Really Happens in *Hamlet?*

It was the accusation that bothered me more than anything else. Miss LePage had said that I didn't have any respect for students' interpretations. "The problem with literary criticism," she had said, just before I fled to the sanctuary of my office, "is that literary critics keep saying the same things over and over again. They're analytical instead of imaginative. No one has said anything new about *Hamlet* in years."

That at least had been her argument in the classroom: literary criticism should be as creative as the work the critic is evaluating. "Some director is always staging Shakespeare in an innovative way—but the critics haven't come up with anything new in ages. So we're stuck with the same old interpretations of the plays."

I had nodded my head in agreement, trying to shut

her up before she went on to something else. She had said too much already. The week before, she had absolutely murdered Spenser's *The Faerie Queene,* suggesting that Spenser's epic poem was a parody of Dante's *Inferno*— with everything reversed.

Four-thirty on Friday afternoon. I sat in the stillness of my office, head in my hands, elbows on my desk, nursing a headache acquired from the class. Outside the door, the hall was quiet. By scheduling one of my office hours from 4:30 to 5:30 each Friday afternoon, I had managed to avoid most of the students who attended my Monday/Wednesday/Friday course in Major British Writers. (I had considered scheduling another office hour at eight o'clock on Sunday morning.) The class itself met late enough in the day that most of the students cut the Friday meeting. The hour in my office each Friday afternoon permitted me to unwind from what was increasingly becoming my most difficult class—largely because of Miss LePage, whose interpretations of late had become so strange that I was beginning to dread walking into the classroom. Frequently, I couldn't sleep; Miss LePage was beginning to reappear in my dreams. And I was smoking way too much, though I noticed that Miss LePage had stopped.

I rubbed my forehead, glanced at my watch, wondering if I simply might go home before the end of the scheduled office hour. Then I listened carefully to the sound of approaching feet, walking down the corridor in the direction of my office. Feminine footsteps—that much I could tell by the sound. When they arrived outside my door and I could see a shadow through the opaque glass, I knew that Miss LePage had come to haunt me once again. The shadow moved, a dark fuzzy arm inched upward, a hand knocked at the door.

I didn't know what to do. I didn't feel like arguing it out with her for another hour, listening to whatever lame-brained interpretation she was bound to have of *Hamlet,* since I had not permitted her to have her say in class. Then the hand knocked on the door a second time.

I contemplated going out through the window, but quickly realized how impractical that would be—it was three stories up. Hide under the desk? Maybe if I didn't do anything she'd go away. Fool—I'd forgotten to lock the door. I sat there in the last rays of the afternoon sun, waiting for the inevitable—waiting for her to open the door. The knob turned slowly, the door opened a few inches, and Miss LePage poked her head in the crack. "I was certain you hadn't left," she said, coming into my office. "Your car's still in the lot."

Embarrassed, I stood up. "I'm sorry. I was thinking—about what you were saying in class actually. Come in." But she was already in, seated on one of the extra chairs in my office. "Was there something else you wanted to say in class, Miss LePage?"

"You didn't give me the chance," she informed me. "Sometimes I think you don't care about our interpretations at all."

"Oh, I do—I do," I told her. "It's just that today there was so much I had to lecture about that I had to cut off the discussion." I knew that wasn't exactly the truth, because Miss LePage was the only student who ever said anything in class. When she didn't reply, I said to her, "Suppose you tell me your interpretation. It's about *Hamlet,* I suspect. Or is it a question?"

"It's an interpretation. My own, of course," she added. "I just thought it's time we had some way of looking at Shakespeare's play that is new, so I sat down last night and tried to find a fresh interpretation."

"And did you find one?"

"I think so—at least I've never heard anyone say this about the play before." There was a long pause. I didn't say anything. Then she spoke again, "Should I begin?"

"Fire away." Visions of her interpretation were already appearing before me: Hamlet was a kleptomaniac, Claudius a fire bug, Ophelia a hermaphrodite.

"The problem with the play, as I see it," Miss LePage began, "is that critics have never figured out who killed the king—Hamlet's father."

"But you have?" I asked her.

"I think so, and one thing is certain—it wasn't Claudius. That's all put in there just to throw us off—the way the clues in any good murder mystery are meant to. It's never the person we most suspect."

"Assuming that that is so, then who did kill the king, Miss LePage?"

"Hamlet."

"Hamlet? Hamlet killed his own father?" I asked her, incapable of holding back my surprise.

"Hamlet—and that, of course, is why the play has always fooled everyone."

"Miss LePage, you know, sometimes I think you haven't read the work we're talking about. Sometimes I think your interpretations make as much sense as if you were trying to figure out the archetypal patterns in the New York City telephone directory—or *The MLA Style Sheet*." I quickly lit a cigarette to calm my nerves.

"What's that?"

"Don't you know what *The MLA Style Sheet* is? And you're a senior in English? Here, take this with you when you leave and memorize it." I handed her a copy of the style sheet. "Now, are you referring to Shakespeare's

Hamlet or William Faulkner's *The Hamlet,* or possibly something else?"

"Shakespeare's Hamlet, who killed his father," she replied.

"In heaven's name, why?"

"So he could be king. Don't you see? It's all a simple matter of power. Hamlet wanted to be king and he didn't want to wait until his father died, so he killed him to speed things up. Otherwise he might have had to wait for years. Don't you see that when we read the play this way, it changes our entire interpretation?"

"I'm certain it does," I replied. "But if Shakespeare wanted us to interpret the play in this manner, why didn't he give us a few clues?"

"Oh, they're all there. It's simply a matter of putting the pieces together."

"And that's what you say you've done now?" I looked at her, wondering why I hadn't told her I had a headache and asked her to come back some other time. "Miss LePage, do you really think that this is the way things happen in *Hamlet?*"

"Well, don't you think it's possible that Hamlet was upset when Claudius became king?" she asked, throwing another question back at me.

"Yes, of course. I agree that much of the play is about that."

"Well, so do I. I'm arguing the same thing. Hamlet is jealous of Claudius and wants him disposed of so he can become king. That's the real shock for him."

"What do you mean? You've lost me, Miss Le Page."

"Hamlet killed his father, never suspecting that Claudius would be crowned king so quickly; but he was, so then he has to kill him off, too. I've worked it out very carefully, Professor. It's a classic case of the Oedipus complex—the same thing that Freud tells us in *Civilization and Its Discontents:* the son kills the father so he can sleep with his mother, but in this case so he can also assume the crown."

"You mean that Hamlet intended to marry his mother once he became king?"

"Well, maybe not marry her, but the relationship he desired was definitely incestuous. She also, you see, throws a monkey wrench into his plans by remarrying rather suddenly. Hamlet didn't know that his mother was playing around with Claudius, and she didn't know that Hamlet was interested in her."

"Miss LePage, I agree that some of this might be possible, but when you start analyzing the rest of the play in these terms, it simply doesn't work. The Ghost of his father, Ophelia, the play-within-the-play—none of these things will fit into your scheme."

"I don't see why not," she answered, a rather determined look appearing on her face.

"Well, what about the Ghost? Why should Hamlet's father's Ghost want to talk to Hamlet if Hamlet had killed him in the first place?"

"That's very simple. It's all rigged. The entire Ghost sequence is planned by Hamlet so no one will suspect that he was the one who killed his father. It's just some guy dressed up as a ghost, pretending to be Hamlet's father. You see, Hamlet can take advantage of other people's superstitions this way. The play-within-the-play amounts to the same thing. Hamlet stages it to throw off both the other characters and the viewers in the audience."

"If that's so, then why does Claudius send Hamlet away to England, Miss LePage?" I asked her, determined to illustrate the absurdity of her interpretation.

"Once Claudius gets the throne, of course, he'll do anything to keep it."

"Why does Claudius eventually admit that he killed Hamlet's father, Miss LePage? How do you account for the scene where he prays?"

"Very easily. I never said Claudius didn't have any guilt feelings. He begins to feel guilty about marrying his brother's wife so quickly. He's all hung up with his own problems of conscience, don't you see? He begins to think he is responsible for his brother's death. I've thought this out very carefully. It all works. Ophelia goes mad because she realizes that Hamlet's not in love with her as she had hoped, but with his own mother. She's particularly upset when he advises her to go to a nunnery. She knows that Hamlet would prefer a more experienced woman. At the end of the play, everybody's so guilty that Shakespeare could find no way out of the mess except to kill them all off."

"In this interpretation, would you say that Hamlet is mad or sane?"

"I'd have to say that he's sane, though because he goofed up in his planning and Claudius became king before he did, I guess you'd have to say that he's mad too—at just about everyone around the court."

"One last question, Miss LePage: What about the whole theory of delayed action, of procrastination? Does Hamlet hesitate?"

"No way. He's the most active character in the play. If he hadn't killed his father, no one would ever have needed to bother about such absurd nonsense. I think it's the critics who have hesitated."

Archetypal Patterns
in *The MLA Style Sheet*

Toward the end of the fall semester, the following essay appeared in my mailbox in the department office:

A.D. 2076

A curious piece of literature, long out of print and forgotten, but recently rediscovered, has of late been the subject of a great amount of debate by a number of literary archaeologists at the nation's archives. Called *The MLA Style Sheet* (1970) by name, this forgotten piece of writing appears at one time—nearly a hundred years ago—to have been held in high critical regard by an obscure group of intellectuals whose followers have long since passed away and whose primary function can at most only be surmised. Yet, the existence of the work itself in what appears to be a second edition, with an initial printing of 250,000 copies, attests to a significance that only years of critical attention may be able to decipher, though within the past few months several literary historians have speculated about the manuscript's significance.[1]

Whatever the origins of this quaint and curious document, its significance as a forgotten piece of literature cannot be denied. The story itself is simple in its elementary complexity, complex in its elemental simplicity, depicting a number of archetypal patterns and situations comparable to other works of the same or related literary form: the *Bhagavad-Gita,* Erasmus's *The Praise of Folly,* and Sir Thomas More's *Utopia.* It is with the last, especially, that a parallel may be drawn, for, indeed, the utopian overtones of *The MLA Style Sheet* (henceforth to be referred to as the *Style Sheet)* are of far-reaching historical proportions—especially when one considers the symbolic ramifications of the document. In truth, the entire narrative may be said to illustrate twentieth-century academe's abortive and final search for an ideal society, a quasi-utopian world of warmth and security. Such, at least, is the literal trajectory of the *Style Sheet.*

[1]The size of the first edition indicates an even more impressive number, approaching a million and a quarter copies in slightly less than twenty years. This phenomenal success, it should be noted, almost equaled that of another contemporary work to which it is thematically related: *Everything You Always Wanted to Know about Sex but Were Afraid to Ask.* (The authoress regrets that this comparison cannot be explored here but must be saved for another article.)

MAJOR BRITISH WRITERS (FALL/SPRING)

The basic narrative pattern of the *Style Sheet* may be said to consist of a quasi-Socratic dialogue between the unnamed narrator (godlike in his omnipotence and power) and the listener to these sacred words. Although the godhead is not named, the listener is referred to quite ubiquitously as the "scholar" or at times "future scholar" or the more lowly "student scholar." Such a distinction, or name as it is used in this case, appears to have marked a strange profession or at least proclivity for some profession, now generally thought to have become extinct. The scholar, who may certainly be considered as a hero figure, undergoes a series of tests and tribulations which, in theory, reinforce the basic initiatory pattern of the narrative. The goal itself appears to be a communion with a third figure—referred to, but never present within the narrative: the professor, editor, or publisher. It is, then, this triangular complexity of the *Style Sheet* that most fully distinguishes it as a work of universal proportions, comparable to the quest motif in *The Odyssey*, *Beowulf*, and other archaic literary works. It is, further, this basic three-cornered situation of student/scholar in pursuit of professor/editor (with the intermediary of the unnamed godhead or narrator) that best illustrates the basic ritualistic overtones of the *Style Sheet* itself (see below).

The quest motif of the *Style Sheet* is in no way, however, limited only to the three-part character relationship (see above). The basic situation of the narrative (perhaps best typified as *picaro-picaresque*), with its multiple hurdles and boons to be overcome and achieved, also illustrates the quest or utopian nature of the work. Part 1 of the *Style Sheet,* for example, "Preparing the Manuscript," is, in essence, a series of rules for pleasing the professor (a cryptic symbol for publication). Not unlike Krishna's advice to Arjoon in the *Gita,* here in the most incipient section of the work itself the lowly student/scholar is given what turns out to be a false sense of security conveyed by such misleading terms as "your editor and publisher," implying, incorrectly, it appears, the ease with which the editor or professor may be reached.[2] It is not until the third section of "Preparing the Manuscript" that the sense of hope and accessibility is diminished with the much stronger statement, *"Never fasten the pages together with more than a paper clip."* (Italics in original.) With this one brilliant sentence, the godhead has warned the would-be student/scholar of the significance that ritual must play in all his endeavors and the necessity of keeping in perspective at all times the conditions under which perfection (the professor or editor) may be attained.

The quest motif is developed throughout the remaining portions of the narrative by the delineation of further ritualistic patterns, designed to illustrate to the student/scholar the remaining obstacles to be overcome before his boon will be awarded. Divisions referred to in the manuscript as "The Text," "Documentation," "Sample Footnotes," and "Abbreviations and Reference Words" culminate in the section entitled "Submitting the Manuscript." This section is then immediately followed by a lyrical description of the utopian goal itself, allegorically referred to as "Proofreading." Always,

[2]This element of internal confusion within the narrative has led several researchers to conclude that the *Style Sheet* may be related to *le nouveau roman;* though one researcher has speculated that the entire work should more rightly be called a *roman à clef.*

however, there is ample warning to the student/scholar that his goal may be attained only by holiness, abstinence, humility, and, above all, by endurance. A recurring motif in all of these sections is the repeated warnings (see above) beginning with the emphatic "never," such as "Never use a comma and a dash together"; "Never use capital 'I' for the Arabic numeral one"; ". . . never send a photocopy or a carbon to an editor unless you send the original as well."

It is, indeed, this distinctly authoritative tone used by the godhead which has prompted recent historical researchers to suggest a religious interpretation for the *Style Sheet,* with those sections of the work beginning with the directive "never" usually interpreted as the taboos of the cult itself. Again and again, it should be noted that the virtuous life suggested by the *Style Sheet* can be attained only by following to the letter those sacred rules and lessons inherent to the basic ascetic life described in the *Style Sheet.* For example, "If students can be persuaded to hand in their papers secured merely by paper clips, they will simplify their own and their instructors' tasks." It is felt that the multiple references to paper clips in the *Style Sheet* are clear indications that the cult itself (at least in its declining years) was anti-machine, perhaps reacting to the encroachment of the staple during the middle and late periods of the last century. These recurring motifs and others related to mechanical technology (as, for example, the recurring image of the typewriter) have led at least one historian to conclude that the entire work should be thought of as the sacred or allegorical writings of a forgotten or extinct religious cult.

Very little is known about the organization which produced the original *Style Sheet* (First Edition) in the year 1951. Literary archaeologists have been almost totally limited in their speculations to that evidence which may be found within the text itself, conjectural as it often appears to be. However, a number of facts and allusions scattered throughout the manuscript suggest that the cult that originally produced the document never achieved majority within the society from which it sprang, even in the years of its strongest following. Estimations of the number of converts belonging to the cult hover around a norm of 30,000 members. It is known, however, from internal evidence within the document, that once each year a sizable number of these converts held an annual synod, and that in late years, just before its demise, as many as one thousand acolytes were ritually sacrificed to the cult itself, in an attempt to purify and strengthen the basic biological unity.

Why did the organization eventually become extinct? About this we can again only sadly speculate. The most frequent interpretation is that the cult itself was incestuous—refusing to accept unorthodox critical ideas—and eventually burned itself out because of a failure to strengthen itself through new bloodlines. Another theory is that sometime in the late 1970s, the cult—which had been patrilineal ever since its origins in the late nineteenth century—underwent a series of schismatic upheavals instigated by its female members in their attempt to impose a matrilineal framework upon the organization. The conflict between these two factions is thought to have led to a bloodbath comparable to that of the Crusades during the Middle Ages.

One curious fact remains for historians to discover—the name of the cult itself—and here the *Style Sheet* offers barely a clue except in the form of a recurring motif as yet undeciphered by literary anthropologists: *PMLA*. This term, or possibly word, was long felt to be an abbreviation for the cult itself. This theory, however, has recently been much in dispute because of the omission of periods after each letter, a practice not used with other abbreviations in the *Style Sheet*. More recent interpretations suggest that *PMLA* (which is used with such frequency within the document that its meaning approaches that of an unknown leitmotif) may be an anagram known only to the cultists themselves. A reversal of the letters (**ALMP**) has prompted one diligent researcher to suggest that what is needed is a basic reshuffling of the letters themselves. If this is done, he claims, they form the word **LAMP**, once again supporting the basic religious and archetypal patterns of the light and knowledge quest implied by the narrative within the work itself.[3]

[3]Note, also, the similarity of *PMLA* and **MLA** in the title of the manual itself. **MLA** when reversed to **ALM** adds further credence to the possibility of a religious basis for the cult.

Return to *Paradise Lost* Revisited

"You know, Professor, you really are the most uptight person I've ever known. I don't understand why you just don't let yourself go once in a while. Sometimes I think you don't even enjoy the literature you teach us."

That was what she had told me in the afternoon—when I'd left her in the library—Clara LePage, the best student in my Major British Writers course, I had decided; the only student I could ever get to contribute to class discussion.

I had gone to the library earlier in the afternoon, hoping to discover something about John Milton, something refreshing that would liven up the following week's lecture on *Paradise Lost*—anything that would offer some new approach to the poem. The last three times I'd taught the course, Milton's *Paradise Lost* had always been the nadir of the semester. Most of the students would sleep through the Monday lecture and then fail to show up for the discussion later in the week, no doubt because they had managed to read only a few lines of the work itself.

Exactly what I expected to find in the library I wasn't certain—perhaps some revelation about John Milton's private life that would shed light on the work itself, some new interpretation of the poem—anything to help make the work "relevant" to today's morass of undergraduate English majors.

"I know the mark of an English major these days is someone who never reads any literature at all," I had told the class the week before. "Nevertheless, I expect that you will continue to read all of the works assigned in this course." It was supposed to be an amusing comment, but no one laughed. Thirty-some students sat there in their chairs, looking at me with hatred in their eyes. So I added, "Or at least have the courtesy to read *Cliff's Notes* before you come to class." That got one laugh—from Clara LePage, the only student who seemed to be awake.

In the library, I looked through the latest *PMLA* bibliography—two years old, of course—in search of that elusive article, that illuminating approach to *Paradise Lost*—but there wasn't anything that gave me the slightest ray of hope. Nothing out of the sixty-seven essays published during the previous year on John Milton in the major scholarly journals throughout the world. Nothing except for an essay called "Fruit Imagery in the Works of John Milton—a Marxist Analysis." But I found that the journal in which the article appeared was missing

145

from the stacks, after I spent an abortive fifteen minutes trying to locate it. Someone else was apparently using it.

When Miss LePage cornered me in one of the stacks a few minutes later, proudly displaying her copy of *Paradise Lost* to let me know that she at least was reading the assigned work, her opening question more than surprised me: "Just what kind of an apple was it that Eve got from the Tree of Knowledge, anyway, Professor?" I could only conclude that she had found the journal I was looking for, removed it from the shelf, and already outmaneuvered me for her next plan of attack in class.

"I guess it must have been a Jonathan or a Winesap," I answered, just the slightest touch of a smile coming across my lips.

"Ah ha, so you can smile if you want to," she replied, her face changing to a broad, uncontrollable grin.

"You ought not to be so hard on your professors, Miss LePage," I replied, continuing before she had the chance to speak. "Are you the culprit who removed Volume III of *Pucred* from the stacks?"

"What are you talking about, Professor? I'm searching for material on Victorian fiction. I think I've discovered a forgotten masterpiece by Patrick Branwell Brontë." I wasn't certain if she was putting me on or not, so I decided to ignore her comment.

"I was searching for an article on *Paradise Lost,* and I thought you might have been reading it yourself in preparation for next week."

"It's all I can do to get through the poem itself," she replied, "though there was something I'd like to ask you about it before we discuss it in class."

"You mean about the apple?" I asked her.

"In a way, yes, though I was just trying to see if I

could get you to laugh for once." I ignored her comment
and asked her what she meant. "I was wondering if that
apple might not have been some kind of aphrodisiac or
something, since, after all, it did get them out of their
dreary anti-sex bag."

"Exactly what do you mean, Miss LePage?" I replied. "Or is this just another of your wild interpretations
concocted to see if you can get some sort of rise out of
me?"

"Not at all"—slipping into a much more serious tone
of voice. "What I'm asking is real enough. I mean, I'd
always heard all these chauvinistic comments applied to
Paradise Lost and everything—that Milton wrote it because he hated his first wife and wanted to get a divorce
from her—but now that I've read it, I can see that that's
not the case at all."

"Well, this is surprising coming from you, Miss
LePage. I think even I would have to admit that the
poem is about the most unflattering picture of women I
can think of for the period when it was written."

"But that's not true, Professor. It's just the opposite. The poem is anti-men and pro-women."

"Have you forgotten that Eve is the one who makes
all the trouble, Miss LePage? The fall of man—because
of the fall of woman," I answered her, rather proud of the
way I had expressed it. Certainly she couldn't accuse me
of being anti-Women's Lib today as she had the year
before when she had been in my American Literature
course.

"You can't be serious about that, Professor," she
continued. "You've got it all wrong. Eve isn't responsible for the fall of man, but rather, for the rise of mankind.
If she hadn't eaten of the apple in the first place, they

147

wouldn't have made love, and then Adam wouldn't ever have been called the father of mankind. I mean, I attribute our whole existence here to the fact that Eve seduced Adam after eating that apple."

"Except that you're wrong, Miss LePage. They had slept together before that apple, you know."

"Well, you've got to admit, I think, that Adam never was really interested in sex until *after* he ate that apple. It's not Adam who's the father of mankind but Eve, don't you see? If it had been left up to him, there'd still be only two people on this earth."

"Miss LePage, are you certain you didn't take that volume of *Pucred* off the shelf? This isn't someone else's interpretation, is it?"

"That's always your way out of everything, Professor—avoid answering the question. Why are you always against an original interpretation of a work of literature?"

I felt as if I'd been slapped. I had come to the library with the express purpose of discovering a new interpretation of *Paradise Lost,* of outmaneuvering Miss LePage, and now that she had given me one, I realized that I had immediately rejected it.

"All of you men—from Adam down," she continued. "Can't you make an objective analysis of Adam and Eve's relationship or at least take someone else's seriously?"

"Go on, I'm listening," I replied, trying to let her have her say. I leaned against a bookshelf.

"Well, you certainly don't think that Adam's very much interested in Eve before the apple, do you?"

"I agree with that."

"It can't have been much of a paradise if there

wasn't any sex there, Professor. That's what's so puzzling about the whole poem. Milton didn't realize what he'd written. He thought of paradise as some place safe, where a male wasn't constantly asked to demonstrate his sexuality. My hunch is that it was Milton who had the real problems. Any woman knows that the paradise came after they got out of the Garden of Eden. Why, until then, there are strong implications that Adam was a homosexual or something. I think he'd have been a lot happier if another male had been made from his rib. Adam acts like a little boy who's had a toy taken away from him—and it's only a rib. My guess is that he's probably afraid to sleep with Eve because he thinks it would be incestuous."

"Miss LePage, you know you really do go a little too far at times. Soon you'll be saying that Adam suffered from penis envy."

"Oh, it wasn't that, Professor. It was simply that for the longest time he didn't know what to do with it." And she disappeared into the stacks with a smile on her face.

Coleridge's "Ancient Mariner"
and Freud's Missing Complex

"All the things you say about 'The Rime of the Ancient Mariner' may be true, Professor, but what makes it relevant for today's reader?" Miss LePage asked.

It was the second half of Major British Writers. For weeks—ever since I had seen her in the library at the end of the previous semester—Miss LePage had been silent in class, and I thought she had been avoiding me. Now I knew that she was back in form. I had spent almost the entire period explicating Coleridge's masterpiece, placing it in its historical context and treating it as a metaphysical reaction to the predicament of early romanticism, symbolic of Coleridge's own repressed Gothic temperament.

"How is the poem relevant to today's reader?" I repeated, rather dumfoundedly, certain that I had already made it perfectly clear.

"Yes, isn't there a better way of interpreting the poem than the way you've done it? I mean—and I'm not trying to negate your approach—don't you think that if we tried to put it into our context today that we might come up with something a little more—shall we say—topical?"

"I thought I had managed to do that, Miss LePage," I replied, naturally on the defensive.

"Well, you did, of course. But what I mean is that academic scholarship today seems to be so narrow in its intent that it never really gets to the crux of what a work of literature is actually about."

"Such as?"

"Well, I went to the library to see if I could find a recent interpretation of Coleridge's poem, and I couldn't believe the limitations of each critic's approach. Someone had written an article called 'Fish Imagery in "The Rime of the Ancient Mariner." ' I was certain that that couldn't be true, but I went into the stacks and located the journal and discovered that the article actually existed. And the poem doesn't even have a thing to say about fish, unless you want to call the slimy things that Coleridge refers to fish, but that does seem to be a bit farfetched."

"So what did you expect, Miss LePage? An article on bird imagery in the poem, perhaps?"

"No, I don't mean that at all. All I'm trying to say is that each critic seems to be pushing—almost trying to sell—his own approach to the poem, or any piece of

literature for that matter, and that's all you can get from
each article. No one talks about the greater meaning of
Coleridge's poem."

"Aren't you talking about varying critical schools
instead of relevance, Miss LePage?"

"Well, possibly, but my whole point is that all criticism seems to be a kind of repression at the base of
everyone else's interpretations except the critic's own."

"Except for Freudian criticism, I suppose," I replied, thinking that I could force her to relinquish what I
expected would be her own approach to the poem.

"No, even Freud. I know what he'd say about this
poem, but I think that even he's way too limited."

"You mean the dynamics of his literary response?"
I couldn't help asking her.

"No, not really. All I'm saying is that Freud, too, is
parochial. He would call Coleridge's poem oral, or anal,
or genital, and that would be the end of that. But how do
we know that Freud was right about those things? No one
ever seems to question his theories—and that's where
the whole thing begins. How did he know that there were
only three stages in our psycho-sexual development?
Why not four or five or two dozen? My feeling is that
there may be all sorts of other stages that Freud never
even thought about."

"Illustrated in Coleridge's 'Rime of the Ancient
Mariner'?" I asked her, trying to bring our discussion
back to the poem.

"Yes," she replied. "It's as good a work as any
other."

"Uh—could you possibly name one of these
psycho-sexual stages that Freud overlooked, Miss Le
Page? I mean, as illustrated in Coleridge's poem, of
course."

"Nasal," she replied, without batting an eye.

"Nasal?" I asked her.

"Yes, nasal—why not?"

"Well, what do noses have to do with 'The Rime of the Ancient Mariner'?"

"I didn't say that you have to have a nose in the literary work itself, Professor. All I said is that the poem illustrates the nasal complex overlooked by Freud. Or in this case, I think we can say a kind of repression of that stage."

"Could you possibly give us a clue?" I asked her. "Just where are these nasal passages, Miss LePage?"

"Well, I think that the first clue lies with the bird itself—the albatross. You know how important a beak is for a bird."

"You mean the pecking order? Aren't you referring now to the bird's oral development instead of its nasal problems?"

"I mean the beak in general—the nose," she replied.

"But wouldn't Freud just as likely call that a phallic symbol instead of a nose, Miss LePage?"

"A nose is a nose is a nose, Professor. No matter what you do with it, it's still a nose. And in the lower creatures, like birds, the sense of smell is more pronounced that it is in man. Any ornithologist will tell you that."

"All of this is most confusing. I guess I don't quite understand what you're trying to tell us. By shooting the albatross, the Mariner was acting out his repressed nasal desires? Is that what the poem's about?"

"No, not exactly. The beak is only the clue. The real intention of the poet becomes apparent when the bird is dead—after he's been shot."

"I think you've lost me, Miss LePage. It's true that the other sailors tie the dead bird around the Mariner's neck, but what does all this have to do with his nasal complex?"

"It's all very simple. If a dead bird were hung around your neck, wouldn't you smell it?"

I realized that it would be better if I didn't answer her question.

"You see, you would. But the Ancient Mariner doesn't. And that gives us our initial clue to the poem's deeper meaning."

"Which is what?"

"That the Ancient Mariner has repressed his nasal desires. He doesn't smell the dead bird or even the entire crew when they're all there lying dead around him. Coleridge even says, when the whole ship is covered with dead bodies, 'nor rot nor reek did they.' So you know that something must be pretty fishy here if the Ancient Mariner doesn't even smell these things. Yet you'll notice that a great amount of detail is spent describing sights and sounds—especially sounds. In fact, the poem is filled up with the noises that the Mariner hears around him."

"Maybe he's at the aural stage and not the nasal stage, Miss LePage."

"You're not taking me seriously, Professor."

"I don't see how I can, Miss LePage. You're doing exactly what you accused the critics of doing—seeing only one thing in the poem. You're so hung up on your nasal interpretation that, if I may hazard a rather far-fetched figure of speech, you've cut off your nose to spite your face. You've forgotten that there is an excellent reason why the Ancient Mariner couldn't have smelled the dead bird around his neck or anything else, so far as that goes."

"Why not?"

"It was too cold. The poem takes place in the polar regions, so he couldn't have smelled anything even if he had wanted to. There was no smell, because the bird was immediately freeze-dried."

"I was hoping you hadn't noticed that." She paused for a moment and then replied, "Well, in that case I'm prepared to retract what I've said—or some of it anyway."

"You're prepared to admit that your theory might be somewhat limited, Miss LePage?" I couldn't believe she had said that.

"Well, in connection with Coleridge's poem anyway. The nasal stage still exists in mankind; it's simply that it doesn't work too well with this poem. I just wanted to try out my theory and see how well it worked. That's not what nosology is all about anyway."

"Nosology? Oh, come now, that means something completely different—the science of classification."

"I know—I checked it out in my *OED*. Coleridge's poem was written so he could depict life in a behavioristic society."

"In a what, Miss LePage?"

"In a behavioral society. That's what's so relevant about it for us today. Coleridge's 'Ancient Mariner' is a study of life in a Skinner Box. But I'll have to explain what I mean next time. The period should have ended ten minutes ago, Professor."

Coleridge's "Ancient Mariner"
and the Skinner Box

"The truth is that Coleridge's 'Rime of the Ancient Mariner' isn't so much Freudian as it is Skinnerian—behavioral," she said, beginning the discussion where she had left it at the end of the previous class.

"Are you trying to say that Coleridge's poem supports B.S.—I mean B.F.—Skinner's theories of behaviorism, Miss LePage? That Coleridge was some kind of precursor of Skinner?"

"I don't see how you can fail to notice that Coleridge is the perfect example of all Skinner's plans for improving the world. 'The Rime of the Ancient Mariner' illustrates all the benefits of behavioral psychology. If Skinner had searched through the classics as Freud did to support his theories, he couldn't have come up with a better example of behaviorism. He might even have invented the Skinner Box earlier than he did. Coleridge's poem depicts life in a Skinnerian environment a hundred and twenty-five years before B. F. Skinner even thought about his box. That's where the real relevance of the poem lies for the modern reader. I'm tempted to send off a copy of the poem to Skinner before he publishes another book. Do you think he'd pay any attention to my letter if I wrote him?"

"I doubt if Skinner reads poetry, Miss LePage. He's not someone like Buckminster Fuller." I expected that she'd return to Coleridge's poem, but she didn't. "I'm afraid I didn't see all this when I read Coleridge's poem, Miss LePage. I wonder if you could illuminate us a little as to how it relates to B. F. Skinner." I looked at the rest of the students, wondering if I should explain to them who Skinner was. Didn't they read *Time* magazine? But, then, it seemed to me that they weren't quite certain who Coleridge was either.

"Well, it's difficult to know exactly where to begin," she replied. "I mean, it's apparent throughout the entire poem—just about anywhere you look, once you really begin to analyze the work in this fashion. I guess I might begin by saying something about the ship itself. Is that all right?"

"Anything that will bring us out of the dark," I replied.

"Well, the physical plant of the community is the ship, a noncompetitive society—or a kind of utopia as Skinner would have us believe."

"A utopia, did you say, Miss LePage? Then why do

so many evils take place in the course of the voyage?"

"I mean utopia in a rather symbolic way, Professor—a kind of ideal world. The dynamics of power have been eliminated here, since the world in Coleridge's poem has moved from a competitive society to a cooperative society. Everyone on the ship has his own particular duty. It's a kind of ideal situation. The power, we might say, has been evenly distributed among all the ship's crew."

"That isn't exactly the normal situation on a ship, is it, Miss LePage? Have you forgotten about *Moby Dick?* If I recall correctly, you saw Ahab as an authority figure."

"But this is different, Professor. 'The Rime of the Ancient Mariner' may be the only piece of sea literature where there isn't any authority figure present. No captain is ever mentioned. No superiors. All the work here has been evenly distributed among the ship's crew. The situation would seem to be completely outside of the possibility of any struggle for power, or any mutiny. It's a world of pure positive reinforcement. That's what I meant when I used the word 'utopia.' Competition has already been eliminated here."

"Then why did the Mariner kill the albatross? Doesn't that seem to contradict your idea? I would say that when the Ancient Mariner kills the albatross, his action reveals that a utopia can't work. It's contrary to human nature. Competition is a basic element in human nature."

"Don't you see what Skinner—I mean Coleridge—is doing, Professor? He's used the ship as an example of stimulus/response. Then when the Mariner shoots the albatross, there's a perfect example of operant conditioning—when the other members of the crew hang the albatross around his neck. You see, the shock of negative reinforcement makes him feel guilty about the crime he committed."

"How can you be certain that the murder of the bird isn't just the result of sublimation of his basic desires?" I asked her. "After all, there aren't any women on the ship."

"Do you mean sex, Professor?"

"Well, yes, what else?" I replied, aware of the fact that I was blushing.

"It could be that, of course. But I doubt if it's that as much as an attempt on Coleridge's part to illustrate that the proper functioning of a community is based upon more than immediate consequences. Usurpation of power is meaningless when there's no power to gain."

"But that isn't what the Ancient Mariner learns, is it, Miss LePage?"

"Well, that and other things, too, because the Mariner survives when all the rest of the crew die off. What good is a utopia when you're the only one left? That's what the Mariner learns, but it's too late—all the others are dead. All he has left to do is to make certain that other people don't make the same mistakes he made. That's why Coleridge has him tell the moral of his tale to others."

"What is that moral, Miss LePage?"

"Environmental control—it's the only chance we've got. That's why he tells the story to the Wedding Guest."

"Now wait a minute, Miss LePage, you've lost me again. What's the Wedding Guest got to do with all this?"

"Don't you see? The Mariner knows he can't get the groom's attention, so he tells the Wedding Guest instead. He's supposed to pass the word on to the groom: Go back to the commune as soon as the honeymoon's over."

Cliff's Notes—
The Archetypal Victorian Novel
by Patrick Branwell Brontë

(Being a synopsis of an unwritten Victorian novel, submitted as partial credit for fulfillment of the requirements for English 213. Section 5. April 4. Clara LePage.)

About the Author

    Patrick Branwell Brontë was the only brother of Charlotte, Emily, and Anne Brontë, the daughters of a Methodist minister. These three sisters composed the literary triumvirate known under the legal name of Currer, Ellis, and Acton Bell Ltd. The Bell sisters have been

treated by literary historians much more sympathetically than their misunderstood brother—no doubt because of the misbelief that they were the ones with the
genuine literary talent in the family—while Patrick, so
the myth goes, was touted as little more than a drunken
sot. The latter belief could not be further removed from
reality. Patrick Branwell was not only the teetotaler of
the family (Emily was high on amphetamines much of
the time when she was writing *Wuthering Heights*), but
Patrick Branwell wrote what critics only in recent years
have recognized as the most significant work to come
from this exceptionally talented literary family—a novel
called *Cliff's Notes,* published in 1843 under the
pseudonym Clifford Bell.

Synopsis: "The Story in Brief "

Clifford Bell was an orphan. His father and mother
died in a carriage accident shortly before he was
born—Mrs. Bell having been undergoing the last pains
of accouchement. But the child, born at the juncture of
two country roads, survived and was brought up by a
cruel maiden aunt, his mother's older sister, named Miss
Loxcomb. In her household, Clifford knew only hardship
and misery. One night—because of enuresis—Miss Loxcomb punished Clifford by locking him in the dustbin.
There Clifford lost consciousness and developed an allergy which was to plague him for many years. Miss
Loxcomb's cleaning woman, Gertie Foote, however,
found him there the next morning and nursed him back
to good health. As a result of the incident, however,
Clifford would never talk to his aunt unless she ad-
dressed him first.

Feeling that Clifford's presence in her house was

becoming unbearable (as a result of the dustbin incident, Clifford sneezed whenever he encountered the slightest bit of lint), Miss Loxcomb made arrangements to send Clifford, now nine years old, away to Heathkit school, a private school for errant orphans, run by three daughters of an ex-Catholic priest: Gondal, Myrtle, and Rebecca Parensell. Clifford looked forward to the new environment with great anticipation.

At Heathkit, Clifford was soon to discover that he was the only pupil of the three kindly Parensell sisters. They had advertised for students in a number of important quarterlies, but only Miss Loxcomb had answered their notices. Here Clifford's days were filled with happiness and contentment—with only an occasional attack because of dust—until his eleventh birthday, when a fever epidemic led to the school's closure: all three Parensell sisters had died.

Determined not to return to his aunt's household, Clifford ran away to Bath, where he became apprenticed to a sadistic masseur known solely as Milhouse. Fourteen hours a day (and sometimes even longer) the eleven-year-old child ran errands for Milhouse, carrying water and washing towels until late at night, when he would fall asleep, exhausted from his day's work. His only comfort was that his allergy had disappeared—no doubt because of the cleanliness practiced in the resort-town massage parlors. Soon, however, Milhouse's constant beatings led to a general deterioration of Clifford's spirits, and he ran away once again—after setting fire to his sadistic employer's outhouse.

Clifford became a street vagabond—without any permanent address. First he joined a gang of beggars in

London, but when their activities changed to thievery, he left them and worked as a bootblack in a carriage house. Next he became a shop assistant for the mysterious Edmund Yorkshire, selling illegal spirits and aphrodisiacs smuggled from the Orient. Still later, when he was nineteen, Clifford became an apprentice mortician to the respected Horatio Balfour, whose daughter, Sylvia, he soon came to love. For three years Clifford worked industriously for Balfour, afraid to propose to the beautiful Sylvia. Then one day, to his surprise, Balfour suggested to Clifford that he marry Sylvia, and Clifford immediately accepted. Tragedy once again intervened—just as Clifford expected his happiness would be complete. On the eve of his wedding, he received an anonymous letter informing him that his beloved Sylvia was expecting a child—by none other than her own father, Horatio Balfour. The secret made public, Balfour hanged himself in his gazebo and Sylvia went mad.

Orphaned again at twenty-two, Clifford thought he would try his luck in the New World. He emigrated to Jamaica, where he eked out a meager subsistence for many years. About to give up in despair, he received a registered letter from Miss Loxcomb's solicitor, informing him of the old lady's demise. On her deathbed she had repented her cruel treatment of Clifford and left him all her worldly possessions. As the novel ends, Clifford Bell, single and lonely, aged forty-three, sits in the spacious library of his plantation home, surrounded by wealth and black servants and his faithful dog Keeper, dictating to his secretary the story of his life, *Cliff's Notes*.

ACADEMIA NUTS

Critical Comment

Because of the date of its publication, Patrick Branwell Brontë's *Cliff's Notes* has come to be regarded as the archetypal Victorial novel, far surpassing in characterization and technical craftsmanship all of the later works published by his three sisters. For years regarded as a *roman à clef,* this tour de force illustrates a number of technical innovations which distinguish it as one of the earliest pieces of experimental fiction. The novel-within-a-novel technique, created by Brontë's decision to have Clifford Bell tell his own story in the third person, confused early readers who thought the book was an autobiography. The picaro-picaresque nature of the plot and its latent gothicism are combined with such skill and subterfuge that *Cliff's Notes* has endured itself to a generation of college undergraduates, whose constant attentions have made it the underground classic that it is.

Browning's Last Duchess
and the Weight-Watcher's Diet

"Do you happen to know how much Browning weighed when he wrote this poem?" she asked, just as I was about to conclude my analysis of "My Last Duchess."

"I'm not so certain that I understand what you're getting at, Miss LePage," I replied, wondering if I was beginning to lose my sensibilities. "Would you mind asking your question again?"

It was getting toward the end of the spring semester, and I thought that Miss LePage was beginning to wind down a bit. She hadn't expressed any of her nitwitted ideas in class in several weeks. I was wondering if she'd exhausted herself on her outside reading assignment on Victorian novels. Possibly it was the senior syndrome—fear of graduating.

"Was Browning given to obesity?" she asked me.

"What in the world does Browning's weight have to do with 'My Last Duchess'—I mean, his last duchess, Miss LePage?" I asked her, knowing that I had probably opened Pandora's Box yet another time.

"I think it may be the key to our understanding his poem," she replied.

"I never thought the poem was that difficult, Miss LePage. It's just a simple story of a duke who does in his first wife because he's jealous of her glances at other men."

"That's the usual interpretation," she replied, "but I think that's too simple. That would be too obvious. Who'd even bother to read the poem a second time if that were the case?"

What was I supposed to say to that? "I've been teaching this poem for fifteen years, Miss LePage, and nobody's ever thought it was anything other than what I've just said. Anyway, Browning is not the narrator of the poem. The duke is, so what does Browning's weight have to do with the whole thing?"

"It's a matter of a kind of subterranean meaning which is clear once you begin looking at the breath patterns of the poem—where the pauses are."

"Ah, yes, projectivism—so you heard the lecture, too?" I replied, referring to one of my colleagues' lectures earlier in the week on projectivism: poetic rhythm, indicated by the natural breathing patterns. The rhythm of a poem is tied up with the natural pauses or breath patterns within the poem. "You've forgotten something,

Miss LePage," I continued. "That theory was developed by a number of contemporary American poets to explain their own work."

"But if it works for them, why can't it be applied to other writers?" And she continued before I had a chance to reply to her question. "A poet with big lungs wouldn't need to take so many breaths, make so many pauses in his poem, right? All I've done is reverse the theory. We ought to be able to read any poem, establish where the natural breaks are (the breaths), and then determine how much the poet weighed."

"What the hell for?" I asked her, losing my patience because she was using up the time during which I had intended to explicate Browning's "Soliloquy of the Spanish Cloister." "Where does all this lead us, Miss LePage?"

"Well, in this poem, to a new interpretation—if you'll let me finish trying to explicate what I mean," she replied, raising her voice a little, or so I thought.

Go ahead and ruin the poem, I felt like saying to her. But all I did was shrug my shoulders and tell her to go on.

"It's all very simple when you realize that the pauses in this poem come about every eighteen or twenty syllables—such as the first one after almost two whole lines: 'That's my last duchess painted on the wall, / Looking as if she were alive.' Now the first pause doesn't come after 'wall,' in spite of the fact that that's the end of the line. It comes after 'alive' instead—eighteen syllables into the poem. And the next breath doesn't come for twenty-two more syllables. So the first thing I think you can conclude is that the narrator of the monologue is a very big man physically."

She stopped for a minute and looked around the classroom at the rest of the students as I lit a cigarette.

"Go on," I said, impatiently looking at my watch.

"Well, here's where this breath approach gets rather revealing. The duke isn't just a large man—he's a huge man—obese, and that's why the duchess can't stand him."

"Wait a minute, Miss LePage," I interrupted. "You're saying all sorts of things that you simply can't prove. Just because the pauses come rather infrequently, you can't automatically conclude that the narrator is a large man."

"Fat, I'd have to call him, so grotesquely fat that his wife commits suicide, since she can't stand looking at him."

"But, but this doesn't make any sense, Miss Le Page. If this were so, if you could determine a poet's weight by the breath patterns in his poems, then—"

"But you can, don't you see? That's the whole thing. Look at Emily Dickinson's poems, for example. All those dashes—every couple of words—whenever she needed to take a breath. My guess is that she weighed about sixty-five pounds."

"Maybe she had only one lung."

"Or Walt Whitman. He had to be a rather large man because of the long lines of poetry he wrote—usually without pauses. Don't you see that I've tried to work this all out logically?"

"But Browning isn't the character in 'My Last Duchess.' He simply uses the duke as the spokesman—"

"Exactly—that's why it's so ingenious. A grotesque monster of obesity—as all the images in the poem suggest, once you begin looking at them in this way."

"For heaven's sake, Miss LePage, you can't do this to a poem. You're distorting Browning's intentions. There isn't one thing to suggest that the narrator is rather—rather large."

"Then why does he suggest to his companion that they sit down while they look at the portrait? Why's there such a big deal made of that unless he's so heavy that he can't stand on his feet for very long? After all, the whole monologue only takes about two minutes, so surely he wouldn't have to sit down if he weren't so overweight, would he? He's got to catch his breath. And then he says, 'I choose / never to stoop.' The fact is that he can't bend over because he's so obese. All his jealousies of his wife relate back to the same thing. He can't ride on her white mule—he can't even get up on top of it."

"So his wife commits suicide because she can't stand to look at him? Is that what you believe the poem's about, Miss LePage?"

"No, not completely. All I'm trying to say is that by looking at the breath patterns here—or in any poem, no matter when it was written—you can learn something about the writer, or in this case, the narrator. Browning's wife, for example, Elizabeth Barrett, was so ill most of the time that she was never able to write anything but sonnets. It was all she could do to get her breath and then spew out fourteen lines before she collapsed."

"Miss LePage, this makes about as much sense as arguing that a poet is right-handed or left-handed based solely on a reading of his poems. Now surely you wouldn't try to do that, would you?"

"No, Professor, that would be too much, although I know some students who feel the university should offer a degree in Left-Handed Studies. Your theory would probably work with painters. Frà Pandolf, the guy who painted the picture of the duchess, was obviously right-handed, and the duke was jealous of him because of that. But that's a theory you'll have to work out for yourself. I can't keep giving you all these ideas. I've got to save some of them for graduate school."

Academia Nuts

It was the last class of the spring semester—Major British Writers, 213—and all I had planned was a general review session, three days before the final examination. I had made some brief comments about recent English poetry and prose, and because of the small turnout (six of the students enrolled in the course), I anticipated that there would be only a few questions. Then I closed my folder of notes, asked if anyone had a question he wanted to ask, and reminded the students to be certain to show up for the examination. "Plan now to attend," I stated before dismissing them. But none of them laughed. I stayed around for another minute to see if anyone wanted to talk to me, but only Clara LePage remained.

"Have you got any suggestions for next semester?" she asked, as we walked out of the classroom and into the hall.

"I thought you were graduating, Miss LePage," I replied, somewhat confused. Had she failed a course? Added up her credits and discovered that she didn't have enough to graduate?

"I'll be coming back in the fall," she replied—with a voice that seemed to indicate that I should have known.

"You're coming back for graduate work? I thought you were joking. Whatever for?" I asked her. "About a month ago you told me that you were tired of English courses."

"That was a month ago. Since then I've done some thinking. I've decided to get an M.A., and then later, somewhere else, maybe a Ph.D. I've got to do something with my degree. The trouble with a B.A. in English literature is that the only thing it's good for is to get an M.A., and once you get an M.A., all you can do is get a Ph.D."

"———?" How was I supposed to reply to that? Never in my wildest dreams (and they had been pretty wild) had I ever thought that Miss LePage might continue her literary studies, getting an M.A. and a Ph.D. I could see it already. In four years she'd expect to be hired by our department. In eight, we'd have to give her tenure. In sixteen, she'd be chairman. Chairperson.

"I thought you might want to recommend some courses for me for next semester, since I told Dr. Turk that I thought you'd be my advisor."

"You could take my course in the Puritans," I replied. "I'll be offering it again, but you'd better register now before it fills up."

"Well, that's not exactly the area I had in mind. I was thinking of something a little more lively, and since I've already had all these other courses with you—" And then she faded off into silence, looking down at the floor as if she wasn't certain she should have made that remark about the Puritans. "Maybe I could be your graduate assistant instead." I didn't know what I should say. We walked slowly down the hall toward my office.

"Perhaps you've stereotyped the Puritans, Miss LePage."

"I haven't done anything. You're the one who's teaching the course."

"I fail to see what that has to do with your remark about wanting a lively course. The Puritans are—"

"But don't you see? The mere fact that you've chosen to teach a course in Puritan literature seems to say something about *you*. I mean, why the Puritans, for Christ's sake? Couldn't you find anything else? Haven't you looked at the other offerings for the fall semester?"

Unfortunately, I had. The catalogue—with its string of crazy course titles—looked as if my colleagues had gone quite mad. "I fail to see what that has to do with my own course, Miss LePage." I noticed that she winced every time I called her *Miss* LePage.

There was a silence, and then she looked me directly in the face and replied, "You are what you teach, Professor."

"I am what I teach?"

"Of course, everyone is."

I looked down the hall to see if anyone was close enough to hear what she had said, but, fortunately, it was empty except for two students standing outside the department office.

"Would you mind explaining what you mean by that remark, Miss LePage?" I stopped walking and tried to move a little closer to her without making it too obvious.

"I mean professors of literature. I don't know if this works with other disciplines. English professors teach the writers they want to be, the ones they think they really are. It's a very simple fact. You can determine an English professor's personality by the courses he teaches. You don't even have to attend a class—just look at the university catalogue and you can automatically tell what the professor of the course is going to be like—his personality."

"Such as?" I asked her, in a considerably lowered voice.

"Well, Professor Stoner's course in Joyce's *Ulysses*, for example. Haven't you ever thought it a little odd that he's so obsessed with that book?"

I had, in fact, but I didn't want to let on to a student what I had thought about it. Professor Stoner's course was called "An Exegesis of *Ulysses*," and he was notorious for teaching only the first few pages of the book—in an entire semester—as if it were *his* work-in-progress, impossible to complete. Some people thought that he had never finished reading the entire book himself. There was a joke going around the department that another colleague was going to offer a course called "A Conclusion to *Ulysses*," with a catalogue description that said, "To begin where Professor Stoner leaves off."

"Haven't you ever noticed the similarities between Professor Stoner and James Joyce? You can never tell what either of them's saying. And they're both practically blind—from the same damn book. If Joyce was the

scholar's pedant, Professor Stoner is the professor's pedant. Why, we spent three whole classes trying to figure
out the meaning of the word 'crossed' in the first sentence. Besides, he's too much of an authoritarian—he
never lets students talk in class, like you do."

"All of this is a little farfetched, Miss LePage."

"Well, then, what about Professor Randall's seminar in Fitzgerald? Surely you must have noticed something a little odd there. The man thinks he's Jay Gatsby.
He's been pining over that woman who rejected him all
this semester."

"I have to confess that I don't know Professor Randall that well," I replied, trying to hold back my as-
tonishment. It was quite a revelation.

"And Ms. Rubens's course in Virginia Woolf. Don't
you see? One of my friends says she's missed six classes
this semester."

I knew what she was referring to. Ms. Rubens, who
had written a book on Virginia Woolf, spent a few weeks
each semester going mad.

"It's all very logical when you start thinking about
these things, Professor."

"Except for one thing," I whispered, afraid she
would lay into another one of my colleagues before I
could stop her. "You're only talking about the professors
who teach contemporary authors. What about Miss Sing-
leton's course in Shakespeare? Who does she think she is,
Lady Macbeth?" I asked, before I realized what I'd said.

"You said it, Professor," she replied. "Don't accuse
me of making any implications."

My mind reeled with other possibilities: Professor
Lee, a true romantic, who taught English Romanticism.
Professor Smith, who taught a course in Elizabethan
poetry which he had recently retitled "The Erotic Fac-

simile," and who was always seducing his students. Professor Bernhardt, who taught "Oscar Wilde and His Circle," and who never gave female students anything better than a C. Professor Goodkind, a little gnome of a man who bored everyone to death, who was a specialist in Alexander Pope. Professor Brown, who taught a seminar in Faulkner and Gertrude Stein, and always repeated himself but never ended a sentence. The possibilities seemed endless: one of my spinster colleagues, who always wore white, spent her life studying Emily Dickinson's poetry; there was Professor Durfman, who taught a course in Spenser's *The Faerie Queene* and was a bit of a fairy himself; and there was Professor Chunk, our ethnic studies dilettante, who had spent a summer at the North Pole and subsequently had written a book entitled *The Submergence of Eskimo Fiction*. Even our well-known psychoanalytic critic, who'd been seeing a shrink for fourteen years and still hadn't learned a thing about himself, but was always recommending his shrink to everyone else. (Four divorces, numerous profligate children, and multiple liaisons with his students—lately both males and females.) I could hardly wait to get back to my office and check the list of fall course offerings.

"You are what you teach," I said aloud to her, as if she were no longer standing next to me. I wondered if that meant you became what you taught or you taught what you had already become. "So what you're trying to tell me, Miss LePage, is that I'm a Puritan?" I looked her directly in the face so I would be certain to detect any changes in her expression.

"Maybe—but this is one of my theories you'll just have to figure out for yourself, Edgar," she said, calling me by my Christian name. And then, before I had the chance to step back, she moved closer to me, kissed me on the cheek, turned around, and walked down the hall, saying, "I'll see you in the fall. Try to get yourself together, all right?"